"You're scared, Mary, aren't you?" Jake asked.

"Of what?" She couldn't take her eyes from his.

"Me, too. I've never felt like this before. I didn't believe it could happen like this."

"What do you mean?"

" 'None ever loved, but at first sight they loved,' " he quoted softly.

"Love." Shock rippled through her. "It's not possible."

"You know what I want to do with you?" he whispered.

She didn't answer.

His hands moved from her hips to her lower spine and began to massage the sensitive hollow. "I want to see that long brown hair of yours against my pillow. I want to touch you until you're on fire for me."

She drew a deep, shaky breath.

"You're so pretty, it's driving me crazy. Come with me to a place where I can touch you."

"It's too soon, Jake. I don't know—"

"If you want to come?" For a moment he looked uncertain. "Don't you want to be with me?"

She should say no. She wasn't the kind of woman who went looking for trouble. But she had no choice. Mary looked up at Jake and a melting sweetness filled her. "Yes . . ."

WHAT ARE *LOVESWEPT* ROMANCES?

They are stories of true romance and touching emotion. We believe those two very important ingredients are constants in our highly sensual and very believable stories in the *LOVESWEPT* line. Our goal is to give you, the reader, stories of consistently high quality that may sometimes make you laugh, sometimes make you cry, but are always fresh and creative and contain many delightful surprises within their pages.

Most romance fans read an enormous number of books. Those they truly love, they keep. Others may be traded with friends and soon forgotten. We hope that each *LOVESWEPT* romance will be a treasure—a "keeper." We will always try to publish

LOVE STORIES YOU'LL NEVER FORGET
BY AUTHORS YOU'LL ALWAYS REMEMBER

The Editors

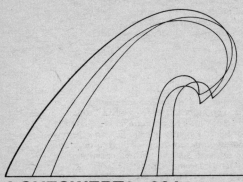

LOVESWEPT® • 364

Iris Johansen
Wicked Jake Darcy

 BANTAM BOOKS
NEW YORK • TORONTO • LONDON • SYDNEY • AUCKLAND

WICKED JAKE DARCY

A Bantam Book / November 1989

LOVESWEPT® *and the wave device are registered*
trademarks of Bantam Books, a division of
Bantam Doubleday Dell Publishing Group, Inc.
Registered in U.S. Patent
and Trademark Office and elsewhere.

If you would be interested in receiving protective vinyl
covers for your Loveswept books, please write to this address
for information:

Loveswept
Bantam Books
P.O. Box 985
Hicksville, NY 11802

ISBN 0-553-22024-1

Published simultaneously in the United States and Canada

Bantam Books are published by Bantam Books, a division
of Bantam Doubleday Dell Publishing Group, Inc. Its trade-
mark, consisting of the words "Bantam Books" and the
portrayal of a rooster, is Registered in U.S. Patent and
Trademark Office and in other countries. Marca Registrada.
Bantam Books, 666 Fifth Avenue, New York, New York 10103.

PRINTED IN THE UNITED STATES OF AMERICA

O   0 9 8 7 6 5 4 3 2 1

One

Said Ababa
April 23, 1986

"Mad, bad, and dangerous to know," Karen Clinton quoted softly, her gaze on the table across the dance floor. "I think I'm in lust."

"You're always in lust," Mary said. Her brown eyes twinkled as she sipped her tea. She didn't bother to turn around and glance across the room. "And you were quoting Lord Byron. Dangerous rakes are a thing of the past. Who is it now?"

"Jake Darcy."

"Here?" Mary had only been home from college for a few months, but even she had heard of Jake Darcy. The man ran some sort of network that was involved with casinos, smuggling, and the sale of information. Not that crime was by any means rare in the police state of Said Ababa, but it was an indication of Darcy's stature in the netherworld that his name was known even to the people who lived on the exclusive upper bank. "Jake Darcy attending a tea dance in a private club? I can't believe it."

"He's with Colonel Pallal and some gorgeous blond. The Colonel must have invited him."

"Colonel Pallal?" Mary stiffened. "Lord, I can't stand that man."

"Who can? He's a creep." Karen gazed again at Mary. "Didn't I see the Colonel with your father the other evening when I picked you up at your house?"

"He's been coming to the house almost every day."

"Why?"

"Some business with my father." Mary lifted her cup to her lips. "I didn't know Pallal did business with the criminal element too. It doesn't surprise me, though." She leaned forward and got back to the subject they'd been discussing before Karen had suddenly noticed Jake Darcy. "Now stop avoiding my question. You have the most gorgeous garden in Said Ababa, and I want it for my kids."

Karen groaned. "Good Lord, two hundred little monsters running around underneath my windows."

"You don't even have to be there." Mary smiled. "This time."

Karen's eyes widened in alarm. "That sounds ominous. I'm warning you, Mary, I *won't* be turned into a do-gooder like you. I don't see how you stand being around all those little guttersnipes any—"

"They're not guttersnipes. They're orphans who grew up in the streets." Mary's voice was suddenly passionate. "They've never had a chance, Karen. You know how rough conditions are in the city. The government's too corrupt to bother about anything but lining the pockets of its own leaders and hacks.

Father Barnard is doing a terrific job of helping the orphans, but he can't do it alone."

"So you're doing your part." Karen shook her head. "No wonder we haven't seen much of you since you got back from school. I'd even heard rumors that you were using your pool to teach swimming when you should have been training."

"We have so much, Karen," Mary said with soft vehemence. "We have to give back."

"*You* have to give back. I enjoy taking very—" Karen broke off and sighed. "Okay, stop looking at me with those big mournful brown eyes. You have the garden." She hastily qualified, "For one day."

Mary smiled brilliantly. "I'll need the household staff to help serve at the party."

"You'll have them." Karen smiled reluctantly as her gaze shifted from the bodice of her friend's white batiste dress to Mary's long brown hair which hung straight and shining to her shoulders. "You look so damned soft and otherworldly that most poeple wouldn't ever guess you have a will of steel." She looked across the room again. "Now that you've dragged me into your drab, do-gooder world, will you please let me reward myself by gazing in peace at that gorgeous man?"

Jake Darcy, Mary remembered. "Be my guest. I have no desire to disturb your libido in any fashion. But I'd be cautious about letting myself fall too much in lust with someone who's involved with that creep Pallal."

She turned and glanced at the table Karen was watching. Pallal's back was turned to them, but Mary recognized his glossy black hair, his mud-green uniform with the scarlet braid. She shivered and her grasp tightened on her cup. Pallal was more than a creep—he was sinister, and the power he held as the head of the secret police made him positively terrifying.

Not that he could hurt her father, she thought quickly. Her stepmother had been a national of Said Ababa, but her father was an American. Though there were no diplomatic relations between the two countries, the Said Ababan government had always avoided antagonizing American residents and visitors.

"Well, doesn't he look like a Regency rogue?" Karen asked.

"Your mad, bad Darcy?" Her gaze shifted to the man sitting across from Pallal and was immediately caught and held. Why, Jake Darcy didn't look like a rogue at all. The only resemblance she could see to Byron were the gypsy-black curls he obviously tried to tame by the shortness of his haircut. His face was alight with laughter and, though his smile wasn't meant for her, she instinctively found her lips curving in response. His well-shaped lips were big and mobile and his eyes, a deeper, keener blue than any she had ever seen, were set in a face bronzed dark gold by the same sun that had formed tiny laugh lines to fan those riveting eyes.

Now he had stopped laughing, but his lips were still quirking as he looked down at his lap. Mary had a side view of the man and of the blond woman next to him. She had rested her hand on his thigh to get his attention, and now, as Mary watched, he covered her hand with his own and began moving it back and forth on his thigh in an intimate caress.

Shock brought hot color to Mary's cheeks. It was the most blatantly sexual act she had ever witnessed in public. She wasn't a prude and heaven only knew that two years at Stanford should have made her shockproof, but there was something about the raw sensuality of the man that jolted her. Then Darcy turned to Pallal and, even as he continued to lazily rub the woman's palm against his thigh, Mary could see him change. Cynicism now dominated his expression; his clear blue eyes were hard and cold. He looked tough, knowledgeable—and Mary could believe he was everything they said about him.

"Well?" Karen asked.

"Lord Byron."

Karen giggled. "I told you." She checked her watch. "I have to run. I have a hair appointment at three. Do you want a lift home?"

Mary shook her head. "I'll finish my tea and then call a taxi."

Karen stood and picked up her purse. "I'll see you at the Parker dinner tonight?"

"Maybe. My dad's been too busy to spend much time with me since I've been home. If I can catch him between appointments I'll send Hajji home, fix my new California burrito supreme recipe and spend the evening with him."

Karen shook her head. "Don't you know we selfish materialistic women of the eighties aren't supposed to be either affectionate or family-oriented?"

A radiant smile lit Mary's face. "Sorry. My father is pretty special."

For a moment the brittle sophistication slipped from Karen's demeanor and she leaned forward and kissed Mary's cheek. "And so's his daughter. It's about time you came home. I've missed you." She straightened. "Well, if papa no-shows you, come to the dinner. You'll be a breath of fresh air in that roomful of phonies."

Mary watched Karen wend her way around the couples on the dance floor and then through the tables to the vestibule. She had missed Karen too while she was at school, but she knew she could never come back to this life when she graduated. No matter how privileged the life-style, living in a police state was not for her. Now that her stepmother was dead, surely her father could be persuaded to give up his interests here and go back to America.

Dammit, she didn't like the fact that Colonel Pallal had been coming to see him so frequently. Her gaze involuntarily went again to Pallal's table.

Jake Darcy was looking at her.

Mary's eyes widened in surprise. Darcy wasn't smiling. He was just staring at her intently, as if waiting for her to recognize him. Recognize? What a crazy impression to have received. She'd never seen the man in her life. She tried to pull her gaze away, and then found she didn't want to look anywhere but at Jake Darcy. Seconds passed and she was still held in that force field of fascination.

Then he smiled at her, freely, joyously, and she found herself smiling back as she had before. She suddenly felt warm and treasured, as if she were wrapped in velvet. Crazy. It was all crazy. What the devil was she doing?

"Ah, your friend has left you. Could I persuade you to join us, Miss Harland?"

Mary looked up to see Colonel Pallal standing beside her chair and she unconsciously tensed. His nondescript, swarthy features revealed nothing but smiling politeness, but she could still sense the sleek menace beyond the courtesy. "Hello, Colonel Pallal."

"My associate, Jake Darcy, is quite taken with

you. He's been plying me with any number of questions and he'd like an introduction. Will you join us?"

She deliberately kept herself from glancing across the room again. "I'm sorry. I have to leave now. Perhaps another time."

Pallal's smile faded. "Darcy is very important to me. I'd appreciate your cooperation."

She met his gaze directly. "No."

Pallal frowned. "You're as stubborn as your father. He's not been overly cooperative either." He bowed. "I hope neither of you regret it. Good afternoon, Miss Harland."

She sat there, frozen, as he turned and left the table and wound his way back across the room. The man had actually sounded threatening. Nonsense— she'd just been telling herself that Pallal couldn't hurt either her father or herself. She straightened in the chair and motioned to the waiter.

After she signed the check, she rose to her feet and quickly left the room.

"No." Jake Darcy was suddenly standing beside her in the foyer. "No, luv, you don't want to go anywhere." He stared gravely at her. "Why would you want to run away from me?"

He spoke with the faintest cockney accent, she noticed absently as she looked up at him. "I beg your pardon?"

"What a polite little girl you are." His hand reached out to touch the shining curve of her hair. "And so clean and pretty. Lord, you're pretty. Pallal just called you Miss Harland. What's your first name, luv?"

"Mary." Dear heavens, she was gaping at him as if she'd never seen a man before in her life.

"I'm Jake Darcy."

"I know. You've become quite well known in Said Ababa in the last few months."

He shrugged. "Well, it's just as well you've heard about me, I suppose. We're over that hurdle." He held out his hand. "Now come back and dance with me."

"No, I was just leaving."

He frowned. "You're afraid of me."

She wasn't afraid of him, but she was suddenly wary of the insane intensity of the attraction she was feeling for him. "No."

He smiled, and she felt the same warmth flow through her that she had when she'd first met his gaze across the room. "It's Pallal; I knew I shouldn't have sent that scumbag over to you. But I knew you weren't the kind of woman a man picked up, and I thought any introduction was better than none."

"I don't know you, Mr. Darcy."

"Jake." His brow furrowed as he stared at her thoughtfully. "Very well. I want you to give me a chance. I think you also want that, but you're too well brought up to give in to your impulses. Ergo, I have to give you a reason why you should do it."

"Mr. Darcy, I don't want to be rude, but I have to leave now."

He snapped his fingers. "The kids. Pallal said you're involved with Father Barnard's charities. Suppose I give you a contribution of ten thousand dollars for one dance."

"Ten thou—"

"Twenty thousand." He smiled beguilingly. "I promise." He held out his hand again. "For charity, luv. Think of those poor kids you can help just by dancing with wicked Jake Darcy."

"I don't think that . . ." But even as she protested she found herself putting her hand in his. A warm tingling began in her palm and started to move through her. She tried to jerk her hand away, but Jake's fingers closed tightly around it.

"Didn't you expect it?" He smiled at her. "I did. It wouldn't be fair to give us the one without the other." He was leading her back toward the dance floor. "I can't wait to hold you. Won't that be a treat, luv?"

"The people at your table—"

"I sent them packing when I saw you getting up to leave."

"That's wasn't very polite."

"It was only business." He wrapped her in his arms and pressed his cheek against her hair. He was a little under six feet and she was a tall woman; they fit beautifully together. "Now, hush and let me enjoy this."

"People don't dance this way in Said Ababa." She could barely speak. She could feel his lean hardness against her as she breathed in the scent of a spice cologne and soap. His hands were resting below her waist, their warm heaviness like an intimate caress. Nothing had ever felt so sexual, so sweet, so *right.*

"I've noticed they're a stuffy lot. Do you suppose they'll ask us to leave?"

"I . . . don't know."

"I hope they do."

"Why?"

"Then we could go home." His lips brushed back and forth against her temple. "Would you like to go home with me, Mary?"

"No. I told you, I don't even know you."

"Yes, you do." Jake's lips grazed the side of her

throat. "You know more about me than I do about you. You know I'm not someone you can take home to mother without giving her a heart attack."

"My mother's no longer alive."

"No? I'm sorry, luv." His tone was perfectly sincere.

"She died when I was three, but my father's still hale and hearty."

He made a face. "I hear fathers are even worse. I think I'll wait until you can't live without me before I tackle papa."

"This is absurd." She promptly nestled closer, belying the words. So right. "We aren't moving."

"That's because I can't dance."

She laughed and lifted her face to look at him. "Then why did you ask me—" She stopped and the breath left her lungs. His face was flushed and his lips were heavy with sensuality. Desire. So intense it aroused an instant physical response. Her breasts ripened, swelled against his chest, and she felt a hot, liquid tingling between her thighs. "Never mind." She buried her face in his shoulder and let him stand there and rock her.

"I don't deal drugs or whores," he said quietly. "I don't sell political or military secrets and I only cheat the people who try to cheat me. I'm not a Boy Scout, but I'm probably better than I'm painted to be."

"Why are you telling me this?"

"Because you have a right to know. You're going to take a hell of a lot of flak." His arms tightened. "But I'll be there to handle anything you can't. Damn, you're so young."

"I'm nineteen."

"That's what I said—so young. When I was nineteen I was a thousand years old."

"How old are you now?"

"Thirty-two."

"Oh, I couldn't tell. You look . . . weathered."

He said dryly, "I am that, luv."

"Are you English?"

"The accent?" He shook his head. "I learned English from a cockney sergeant in Malaya when I was a kid."

"You were in the army?"

"Several armies. I was a mercenary from the time I was fourteen." His lips brushed her ear. "Not a pretty picture, eh?"

"Fourteen?"

"I had to make a living. I have a fondness for eating."

"What about your parents?"

He shrugged. "Who knows? I grew up in the streets of Bangkok." He looked soberly down at her. "I can't give you any kind of guarantee of pedigree and I'm not making excuses. If you have problems with that—"

"Pedigree?" She looked up at him with a frown. "What kind of narrow-minded bigot do you think I am?"

His lips curved in a rueful smile. "Well, look where we are, luv. I couldn't believe it when I walked in here. A tea dance! I thought they went out in the twenties. All soft music and low lights and well-bred voices. I knew the minute I walked through the door that Pallal had brought me here to intimidate me." He drew her close again. "And then I saw you sitting there in your white dress, looking like a good little girl all ready to go to Sunday school. You belong in a room like this."

"Bull." Mary grimaced. "And I wish you wouldn't keep referring to me as a good little girl."

"I think you're probably a very good little girl." His eyes twinkled as he looked down at her. "I bet you keep your room tidy and visit Auntie Marge every week even though you can't stand her and go all softhearted when you see a stray dog or cat."

"I don't have an Aunt Marge."

"But the rest is right?"

She wrinkled her nose. "They say the face we're born with influences our personality. I know I look as wholesome as hot milk and Grandma's cookies, but I'm not really—"

"I like hot milk."

"No one likes hot milk."

"Then I like Mary Harland. I'd wager everybody likes Mary Harland."

"Only mothers and grandmothers. Wholesome is definitely not in this year."

"It should be."

"Not according to—" She broke off as she gazed up at him. She felt the heat move through her and she stood there staring helplessly at him as they rocked slowly back and forth.

"Mary?"

She shook her head and laid it in the hollow of his shoulder. Her cheeks were flushed; her entire body felt flushed, aching with a strange sensitivity. They were so close she could feel the intake of every breath he drew, and she felt somehow joined to his every response. They didn't speak for a long time and with every moment she felt the intimacy thicken, her response to him heighten, until she actually began to tremble. What was happening? She felt as if she were melting.

"I . . . like that song they're playing. My father has a tape of it by Frank Sinatra."

"I've never heard it before."

"It's 'Softly As I Leave You.' "

The hushed, melancholy strains of the song wound around them, weaving ribbons of emotion as they moved to the music.

"What are the words?" Jake's question was a warm whisper in her ear.

"I don't remember. Something about a man leaving his lover and being afraid she'll wake before he goes."

"I don't think I'd like it. The man's obviously a bloody fool."

"Not to want to wake her?"

"To leave her at all. A man should hold on to what he wants." His arm tightened around Mary's body. "The tune's pretty, though. We'll go with the music and jettison the words."

"Will we?" The music, his words, the feel of his body were all weaving a spell as sweet as the song itself. "I think . . . I'd better go."

"You're scared." His lips touched her temple. "Me, too. I've never felt like this before. I didn't believe it could happen like this."

"What do you mean?"

" 'None ever loved, but at first sight they loved,' " he quoted softly.

"Love." She felt a shock ripple through her and shook her head. "Not love. In spite of what Shakespeare says there's no such thing as—"

"Chapman."

"What?"

"It's George Chapman. It's a quote from *The Blind Beggar of Alexandria*, 1598."

She was immediately diverted. "You like poetry?"

"I do like it, but actually I'm something of a fraud. I couldn't learn how to read, so I bribed one of the sergeants to repeat an eight-hundred-page book of quotations over and over to me. Before the campaign was finished I'd memorized the whole bloody book." He grinned. "You'd be surprised how impressive a one-liner deftly inserted in exactly the right place can be."

"Why didn't you bribe him to teach you to read instead?"

"I have dyslexia. Of course, I didn't know that at the time. I thought there was something wrong with my head. It wasn't until I quit the service that I found out there was a cure for my problem."

But he had overcome the handicap, as he had his childhood. Mary shook her head. "Amazing."

"Have I impressed you? Good. That was my intention. It never hurts to have a little respect mixed into the chemistry."

He drew her closer and she immediately forgot about everything but the chemistry itself. She couldn't stop trembling, she realized dazedly. Her knees felt filled with fluid and she was glad he was holding her or she might have fallen. She felt torn from everything she knew, isolated, incomplete. She could feel the hard column of his manhood pressed against her, and it didn't shock or frighten her. Instead, it brought her a sense of comfort: Jake could take away the isolation. He could complete her.

"You know what I want to do with you?" he whispered.

She didn't answer.

His hands moved from her hips to her lower spine

and began to lazily massage the sensitive hollow. "I want to see that long brown hair of yours against my pillow."

She drew a deep, shaky breath.

"I want to take off that nice white dress and see you naked in my bed. I want to look down at you and know you're waiting for me to come inside you."

Heat rushed through her, her breasts swelling in response to the word picture he drew. She could see Jake looking down at her with those intent blue eyes, his lips as sensual as they were now as he smiled at her.

"I can see you." His chest was lifting and falling with the force of his breathing and she could feel the hotness of his body through the clothes separating them. "I can see myself pushing your legs apart and looking at you. You'll be so pretty, and it will drive me crazy knowing I can reach out and—"

"Jake!" Her voice was low, strangled. She could see it too. She could almost feel his hot, intimate gaze on her.

"Do you like this place?" he asked thickly.

A ripple of tension went through her. "Not really. I used to come here before I went away to college and there's usually someone I know here, but—"

"Thank heaven," he said fervently. "Come on, let's get the hell out of here." He grabbed her wrist and started propelling her across the room.

"But I don't know if—"

"We don't have to go to my place. I just have to take you to a place where I can touch you."

"Jake, it's too soon. I don't know if—"

"If you want to come?" He stopped abruptly at the doorway. For a moment he looked uncertain. "Don't you want to be with me, Mary?"

She should say no. This physical attraction was too strong, too erotic, his personality too dynamic. She wasn't the type of woman who went looking for trouble. She was sensible and had goals to meet. She looked up at him and felt a melting sweetness rippling through her. "Yes."

She was rewarded by a brilliant smile. "I'll go slow. I won't take anything you don't want to give. I know I shouldn't have come on so strong back there. I just didn't have much time and I had to make you see the possibilities."

"You did that." She smiled tremulously.

"I was inspired." He propelled her out into the car park and then toward the black Mercedes a few spaces away from the front entrance. "It shook me up too." He opened the car door and helped her into the passenger seat. "I always thought it was bull."

"What?"

He slammed the door and got into the driver's seat. "All that bit about love at first sight." He met her gaze and smiled. "But it isn't, is it, luv? We've got it good and proper."

He was saying it again. "It's not love. I've known you for less than an hour."

"But you like to be with me? You don't want to let me out of your sight? That's the way I feel."

"Sex?"

"Uh-huh." He shook his head. "Lord knows that's there too. If you weren't such a good little girl I'd have been tempted to make love to you on that dance floor." He leaned forward and kissed her cheek. His lips were warm, sweet, loving, enfolding her in that same velvet cloak of treasured protection promised by his smile. He leaned back and drew a shaky breath. "Not yet. You have to see that there's a hell of a lot more." He put the car in gear and backed out of the parking lot. "Talk to me. Tell me about yourself."

"I thought Pallal told you all about me."

"Not enough."

"What do you want to know?"

"Why are you in Said Ababa? It's not the kind of place any American would choose willingly."

"My father came here on business ten years ago and fell in love with a Said Ababan woman. The government wouldn't give Rillah an exit visa so Daddy moved us here. He never regretted it for a minute, until Rillah's death last year."

"And you didn't object?"

"I liked Rillah," she said simply. "She was kind to me and made my father happy. Why should I object?"

"I imagine a number of children could find reasons."

"It wasn't a bad life. I didn't really know what I missed until I went to the States to college two years ago."

"Pallal said you were trying out for the Olympic swimming team this year."

She nodded. "I probably won't make it. I keep getting distracted by other projects."

"What are you studying?"

"Art, with a minor in business. I want to be a jewelry designer. My father's David Harland. Perhaps you've heard of him?"

He gave a low whistle. "Harland Jewelers. New York. London. Paris. He owns one of the finest jewelry collections in the world. Your daddy's loaded."

"That sounds pretty snobbish."

"I have no objection to money. I plan on being rich as Croesus myself. However, the fact that you're rich just puts another obstacle in our way. Are you and your father close?"

She nodded and smiled. "He's terrific. Kind, gentle, understanding."

"I guarantee he wouldn't understand you being with me today," he said dryly. "And I don't think you'd lie to him."

"No, I couldn't do that." She looked at him, troubled. "Would you want me to lie?"

"Personally, I'd take you any way I could get you." He glanced at her. "But I'm glad you're honest. No, I don't want you to lie, luv."

Mary moistened her lips with her tongue. "I don't know about any of this, Jake. It complicates everything."

Two

Jake pulled into the underground parking lot beneath the high-rise apartment building and coasted down the ramp.

He parked directly in front of a bank of elevators guarded by a huge, burly man dressed in an immaculate dark business suit. "That's Bruno." Jake grimaced. "He doesn't like me driving into the parking garage without someone around."

The man grinned at Jake and made a sign that everything was okay.

"A bodyguard?" Mary looked at Jake, startled.

"It's not your world, is it, luv?" Jake shook his head. "I had my plan of operation all worked out. In five years I was going to go completely legitimate and retire to Switzerland with enough money to make me palatable to even the most discriminating social set. Now, I may have to escalate the agenda." His hands tightened on the steering wheel. "You don't have to come up with me. If you do, we're probably going to end up in bed. I'll want to make sure of you any way I can."

The silence was fragile, fraught with crystals of emotion and yet thick with that same overpowering velvet sensuality that had swept her toward him from the first moment he'd smiled at her. She felt the muscles of her stomach clench as she looked at his long fingers grasping the steering wheel. He would touch her with those hands. She already knew his touch, the feel of his body pressed to her own, and she would know it again in an even greater intimacy if she went with him. He wouldn't force her; he was giving her a choice. She could refuse to go.

No, she couldn't refuse, she knew suddenly. She had no more choice than she had had in that first moment. The rapport was so strong she could almost believe Jake was right and that it was destiny that had brought them together. They'd both been drawn into a vortex of feeling that wouldn't release them no matter how hard they struggled. She wasn't sure that she even wanted to be released now. She drew a tremulous breath, opened the door, and got out of the car. "Introduce me to Bruno."

His smile was radiant. "You bet." He was out of the car and beside her in minutes. His hand closed around her own as he led her toward the elevators. "Bruno Wizkowski." He unlocked the elevator. "This is Mary Harland, Bruno."

"Delighted." Bruno's voice was deep and cultured, in complete contrast to his massive wrestler's physique. "I hope to see you here again, Miss Harland."

"Thank you," Mary smiled at him. "I've never met a bodyguard before. Is it an interesting job?"

Bruno shot a wry glance at Darcy. "It has its moments. Depends on the client."

The doors of the elevator slid open and Bruno glanced inside before permitting them to enter.

"He seems very pleasant," Mary said as the elevator doors closed and the elevator started to rise. "But do you really need him?"

"Yes. Said Ababa is one of the most corrupt countries in the world. Not that I should complain. It's the kind of climate where an enterprising bastard like myself can make a bundle."

"I saw you with Colonel Pallal. I don't like him."

"Neither do I. The bastard wants a monthly cut of the take of my casinos."

"Are you going to give it to him?"

"No, but he won't find out until I'm ready to tell him."

"When will that be?"

"When I've discovered something he doesn't want his superiors to know about. Bruno's working on it now."

"Blackmail."

"It's the way the game's played here."

She shivered, and his hand tightened on hers. "I don't want to talk about Pallal. Who was that woman at the table?"

"One of Pallal's agents." Jake grimaced. "You saw that little byplay? He brought her to show me the fringe benefits of becoming his partner."

"She seemed very eager to please." Mary heard the edge in her tone and hurriedly added, "I'm sorry, it's none of my business what you—"

"The hell it's not." He pulled her against him and his mouth closed on hers, quick, hard, and hot.

"*I'm* your business. And you are mine. Just you. Okay?"

"Okay." She didn't even know she'd said the word. She couldn't breathe. The heat of his body, the *feel* of him sweeping through her, melting her, as it had done on the dance floor but stronger, unbearably so. . . . She could feel his arousal pressed hard and bold against her lower body. She moved closer and her mouth opened to receive him.

He groaned low in his throat as his tongue invaded her. His hands moved down and cupped her buttocks as he moved her against his lower body. "Sweet, luv." He was trembling against her, his face flushed. "Give me—" His mouth closed on her tongue, sucking.

He was unbuttoning the pearl buttons on the front of her dress. "I want to see you. All right?"

He didn't wait for an answer, but parted her dress and unfastened the front hook of her bra. She couldn't have answered anyway. Her knees were so weak she was having trouble standing and she had to hold onto Jake's shoulders to keep upright.

"Like pretty apples." He was looking at her breasts, and a hot shudder ran through her as she saw the intensity on his face. "Small and sweet and just right." He lowered his head and his mouth closed on her right breast. "*You're* just right for me," he said thickly as he lifted his head. "All of you. I want to be inside you so bad I'm hurting."

Her hands tangled in hair. She swallowed and then cried out as his teeth closed gently on her nipple.

"I didn't hurt you?" His hand lifted in concern and then he smiled as he saw her scarlet cheeks and dazed expression. His palm moved down and began to rub back and forth against her womanhood. She arched back against the gleaming Formica wall of the elevator. "Jake!"

"I know." He took a step toward her and started to lift her skirt. "Come here. Let me—" He stopped and put his arm around her waist. "Not in the elevator. Come on."

When had the elevator stopped, she wondered dazedly. The doors were open and entered directly into the living room of a suite, but the furnishings were only a blur of color to Mary as Jake swept her across the room and into the bedroom.

His hands were shaking but lightning-swift as he undressed her and then himself. His eyes were glazed, wild, as he tore off the last item of clothing. He was frantic, but so was she. She couldn't get close enough fast enough.

He pushed her back on the bed and parted her thighs, immediately pressing against her. "This isn't how I planned it," he muttered. "Mary, luv, I have to—"

Pain!

She cried out.

Jake looked down at her. "Lord, Mary, what the—"

"Never mind." She was moving, surging, frantic to keep him within her. "Jake, *help* me."

"Easy." His hands gentled her, even as he began to move with a rhythm that was as frantic as her own. "I'll help you. I'll help you, baby."

Their joining was wild, urgent, as insanely erotic as the attraction that had brought them together. He couldn't get enough of her. She couldn't give enough to him. The intensity was so great, it couldn't last long. The explosion came with a primitive force that left Mary weak and shaking in the aftermath. She lifted a trembling hand to push back a lock of hair that had fallen over her eyes. Her heart was beating so hard it was painful.

Jake was looking down at her in concern. "Okay?"

She nodded breathlessly. "You?"

He nodded. "Other than feeling like I've been through a hurricane." He kissed her lingeringly. "Stay there."

He moved off her and she immediately felt a strange sense of desolation. He walked across the room toward a mirrored closet and she watched him in a languorous haze. Tight buttocks, muscular thighs and calves all moving with a well-oiled smoothness. He glanced back over his shoulders with a grin. "Hey, what you looking at, mate?"

"You. I've never see a naked man except in the movies."

His grin faded. "So I found out." He was coming back to her with a white terry-cloth robe in his hand. He sat down and draped the robe about her shoulders. "Sorry about that, luv. I would have been more careful if—" He ruefully shook his head. "No, probably not. I was so crazy for you."

"I know virgins are an endangered species. It was time I joined the twentieth century."

"Yes, it was time." His hands cupped her cheek. "But Lord, I'm glad it was with me." He kissed her slowly, lingeringly. "I don't suppose you're on the pill?"

She shook her head and then burrowed her face into the crook of his shoulder. "I should have said something."

"I didn't give you much chance." His hand was gently massaging the muscles of her neck. "I'll protect you next time, luv." His tone was gruff. "If you want to be protected. I don't give a damn if we have a kid. Whatever you want. . . ."

Children. He was talking about children and they had only just met. The world was turned topsy-turvy, and all because she had looked up and seen Jake Darcy across the room. "Not yet." Her voice was muffled against his shoulder. "It's too soon. I'm all . . . unbalanced."

"Me, too." His thumb rubbed soothingly at her nape, smoothing out all the tension. "I realize you don't know what to think about me, about this. I know you'd never have let me love you, if we hadn't both gone crazy with wanting each other. I meant to give you time to get used to me." He tilted her head back to look into her eyes. "Just don't back off from me now. I couldn't take it, Mary."

She laughed shakily. "You don't see me running out the door."

"It wouldn't do you any good. I'd call down and have Bruno stop you."

Her eyes widened in sudden apprehension.

He shook his head. "I was joking. I don't have Bruno force women to stay in my bed." He frowned. "Hell, you should have known that."

"I don't know anything about you."

"But you should have realized I'm no—" He made a face. "I'm expecting too much. Come on. Into the shower with you." He pulled her to her feet and draped a companionable arm around her waist as he walked with her toward the adjoining bathroom. "You may be a little sore. This kind of sport is new to you." He winked. "Though I'd say you have a fantastic talent for it. I'll call down and have Bruno order us some dinner. It's a little early, but I suddenly have a voracious appetite. What would you like?"

It was only a little after six, she realized with surprise. "Anything."

Jake was carefully adjusting the water in the shower stall. "I'll choose then." He took the robe off her and pushed her gently under the spray. "I'll be right back." The frosted door slid closed.

She stood dreamily under the warm flow, her mind blank to anything but the sensual pleasure of the gentle spray. Jake had done everything for her with a loving care and tenderness that made her feel valued and cosseted. It was strange how she could accept every intimacy he extended with such a feeling of supreme naturalness. She should be shocked, she thought, at her own behavior, and apprehensive of the intensity Jake was displaying in forging their relationship. But she felt neither shock nor apprehension, only this sense of mellow rightness.

The glass door slid back and Jake stepped into the shower. "Lobster okay?" He closed the door behind him and took her in his arms. "And vanilla ice cream. I love vanilla ice cream."

"Fine." The spray was enveloping them both in warm intimacy and Jake was holding her sexlessly, lovingly, companionably. "I like chocolate better though."

"Next time we'll have chocolate."

'Next time.' Jake said the words with such certainty that she could almost believe that there would be a next time and that tonight wasn't just a halcyon dream. She closed her eyes and stood there with him under the spray while he rocked her gently back and forth, the way he had on the dance floor.

"Mary?"

"Hmm?"

"We have to get out of here." There was a thread of tension in Jake's voice and a renewed urgency in the manhood pressing against her. A thrill of hot need went through her. Again. It was here again. Urgent. Frantic. He added thickly, "Now."

"No." Her fingers dug into his shoulders. "Here."

"I have to protect—" He shuddered as she pressed closer against him. "You said—"

"I don't care." She moved slowly back and forth against him. "Jake . . ."

He lifted her, adjusted and sank home. "Oh, love," he whispered. "Oh, my dear love."

It was nearly midnight when Jake parked the Mercedes in the driveway of the imposing brick mansion. "Very posh," he said without expression. "The best neighborhood, the best clubs, the best schools."

"You're being snooty again." Mary leaned forward and kissed his cheek. "I can't help it if Daddy's rich, and I certainly don't intend to apologize for it."

"I'm not going to let you go, you know," he said quietly. "I have no intention of being a one-night stand. When do I see you again?"

"Tomorrow. I'll come to your apartment at three."

"A spot of sex in the afternoon before tea?" He shook his head. "Not good enough, luv. I want to meet your father."

Mary felt a surge of panic. "Not yet."

"Why not?"

"Let me prepare him."

Jake's expression hardened. "For me?"

Mary looked at him with exasperation. "For heaven's sake, Jake, you told me yourself that you knew he wouldn't approve of you. I love my father and I'm not going to hurt him."

He looked at her for a moment and then nodded slowly. "Okay, I'm being unreasonable. I've never felt like this before and I'm scared as hell. How long?"

"How do I know?"

Jake's hands cupped her shoulders and he stared into her eyes. "How do you feel about me, Mary?"

"I . . . I don't know." She felt her eyes fill with tears. "I'm confused. You're not what I wanted for myself. I wanted someone solid and steady." She laughed shakily. "You're hardly a solid citizen."

"But I'm steady. No one could ever be more steadfast than I'll be for you."

"I know. That's why I'm so mixed-up. You don't fit in any pattern. You're kind and you're so good to me and you make me feel as if I never want to leave you again." She drew a trembling breath. "And you know how you make me feel in bed."

"Isn't that enough?"

"I don't know you. I'm even a little afraid of you. I need time to adjust." She cupped his hard cheek in her hand and felt that poignant, melting sweetness move through her again. "But I don't think I can ever be happy without you, Jake."

He turned his head and kissed her palm. "I'm going to make damn sure you never get the chance," he said thickly. "You know, half the world believes in destiny. I never thought much about it until tonight. But, dammit, I believe we were meant to be together. I *know* that if we hadn't met today, we'd have met at another time or place. So don't think you're going to get away from me." He licked her palm and felt the responsive shiver that went through her. "Get inside or we'll be trying out the backseat of this Mercedes. I'll see you tomorrow afternoon."

She scrambled out of the car.

"I'll send the check to Father Barnard tomorrow."

"What?"

"I promised you I'd send a check to help the kids if you'd dance with me."

She had completely forgotten the method he'd used to persuade her into his arms at the club. Not that she'd needed much persuasion, she thought ruefully; he was right, she'd only needed an excuse. "It wasn't a line?"

He looked at her in surprise. "I keep my promises, Mary. Always."

"Twenty thousand dollars is a good deal of money."

"It's a good cause. I can identify with the need of street kids."

Because he'd been one himself, she thought compassionately. "Yes, it's a damn good cause." She slammed the car door, waved, and then searched through her bag for her key as she climbed the six steps to the front door. She smiled as she realized Jake was waiting for her to get inside before he left. She had found out even in this short time that one of Jake's principal characteristics was a possessive protectiveness. It was a quality she found both endearing and heartwarming. She unlocked the door, waved again, and entered, closing the door behind her. Immediately she heard the engine of the Mercedes through the oak door.

The hall was dark, but there was a light beneath the door of her father's study. Working late again, Mary thought with concern as she moved toward the door. He should get more rest. He'd been looking haggard lately.

"Okay, Daddy, time to give it up for the night," she said as she threw open the door. "Don't you know slavery's been outlawed even in Said—"

"Good evening, Miss Harland," Rustin Pallal said as he got up from the big easy chair across the room. "I've been waiting for you."

"What do you mean? Daddy, what—" Her gaze turned to the desk where her father sat. "*Daddy!*"

Three

"You should have left Said Ababa three days ago," Bruno said gloomily, gunning the accelerator. The jeep lurched and then flew down the desert road toward the city of Tarbol. "Pallal is going to have your guts for breakfast."

"Then he'll have a profound case of indigestion," Jake answered as he leaned back against the seat of the Jeep. "The good Colonel's found me less than palatable before in our dealings." He shot an amused glance at Bruno. "You worry too much. Pallal's not going to throw me into his jail until he's sure I have enough liquid assets on me to make it worth his while. My guess is that he'll try to pick me up at the last minute before we depart this land of milk and honey. And, as he doesn't know how we intend to leave, he must be frustrated as hell right now."

"You should have been on that yacht the minute you got rid of your assets here." Bruno glanced at the backseat, where a small Chinese man was sleeping. "Chen was in a damn sight less danger than you are."

"Chen works for me, and I take care of my own. Once I leave the country there's going to be a scrambling to snap up everything I've left behind. Pallal will strike out at everyone who was close to me. It's the way he works. He'd like nothing better than to have me know he had Chen in one of his security prisons." He grinned. "Now, you know it's far more sensible to bring Chen with us than to have to break him out of jail in six weeks time, mate."

Bruno nodded reluctantly. Chen, the manager of one of the casinos near the oil refineries, was only a minor figure in Jake's organization, but Jake had built that organization on mutual trust. In a world where loyalties changed with the blowing of the wind, Jake stood rock firm. If you worked for Jake, you performed your job with unswerving loyalty. Nothing else was accepted and any deviation was met by instant punishment. In return, you got a fair shake, a damn good living, and all the protection Jake could provide.

"You know we've been followed by Pallal's goons for the last four days?"

"Yes, but I haven't seen any sign of them since we picked up Chen. Curious."

"We're still being monitored. I saw a state helicopter about ten minutes ago."

"Once we reach the Casbah we'll lose them."

"But you'll leave tonight?"

"Tonight." Jake stretched out his long legs. "I'm

looking forward to St. Moritz. I'm tired of this heat. I think I'll teach you to ski, Bruno."

"Me?" Bruno looked at him, startled. "On those little slats? I can think of other ways I'd rather risk my neck."

"Like working for me?" Jake chuckled. "But I'm legitimate now, Bruno. We'll have to find you some other occupation to amuse you."

"You still have enough enemies floating around to keep us all busy for a decade or so," Bruno said grimly. "I'll stay off the skis, thank you."

"Whatever pleases you, mate." Jake closed his eyes and lifted his face to the night breeze.

As long as it also pleased Jake, Bruno thought resignedly. He was completely relentless when he made up his mind. He'd use charm and charisma and every cell in that brilliant, innovative brain to bend circumstances to his will. So, Bruno thought, he would probably end up on those damn skis and Jake would see that he enjoyed the hell out of it. Well, why not? He was glad to see Jake finally returning to his old self. He hadn't seen him this lighthearted in the three years since Mary Harland had died in that damn plane crash.

"If you don't like snow skiing, we'll have to try hang gliding," Jake said without opening his eyes, his expression deadpan. "Flying over the Alps is supposed to be quite—"

"Skiing," Bruno said quickly. "No hang gliding. Skiing."

A smile lit Jake's face as his eyes opened. "Ah, you'll love it, mate. Gliding down the slopes. The wind—watch it!"

A woman was standing in the center of the road!

Bruno, too, had seen her. He swerved the Jeep off the road, the wheels sinking into the sand. The beams of the headlights danced crazily over the dunes in the distance as the Jeep shuddered to a halt.

Jake was quickly unbuckling his seat belt. "Idiotic woman. We could have ended up overturned with our heads bashed in. She must be on something. Hell, why should she be any different? The whole damn country is opium heaven." He was striding toward the woman, who was still standing in the deeply shadowed road.

Chen raised himself to a sitting position in the backseat. "That's not the way a man wants to be awakened, Bruno."

Bruno unwound his large frame from around the steering wheel. "Is she okay? I didn't hit her, did I?"

"It wouldn't have been your fault if you had," Jake said. "Listen, lady, if you want to overdose on hashish and kill yourself that's your business, but keep out—"

The woman swayed and fell to the ground.

"What the hell! Get a flashlight and the first-aid kit, Bruno."

"I hit her?" Bruno turned and reached under the seat. "Damn, Jake, I swear I didn't feel a bump."

"We'll soon see." Jake knelt by the woman. "I think she's unconscious." The woman was lying on her side, her bare arms lax. She was dressed in ragged dark pants and a tunic top. A wild cloud of bushy dark hair veiled her face.

Bruno turned on the flashlight as he knelt beside Jake. "This would have to happen now. You can't get involved, Jake. We'll take her to the clinic on the way to the harbor."

"No."

"What do you mean no? Pallal will—"

"Look at her arm."

Bruno brought the flashlight closer to the woman's outflung arm. A two-digit number was tattooed on the wrist. "Balahar." He felt a rush of pity. She was a prisoner from Balahar, Pallal's pet security prison for political prisoners. Horror stories abounded of the tortures and deprivations of Balahar.

"Do you think Pallal released her into the desert to die?"

"Have you ever heard of Pallal releasing a prisoner? She must have escaped somehow. Heaven only knows how. The prison's over twenty miles from here." Jake held out his hand. "Give me the canteen."

"Burgundy . . ." The word was spoken softly, a mere breath of sound coming from the woman's lips. "Burgundy . . ."

Jake stiffened as if he'd been shot. Bruno's gaze flew to his face. Jake whitened in shock; a muscle jerked in his jaw.

"Jake?" Bruno asked.

"Turn her over," Jake said hoarsely.

Bruno carefully lifted the woman and placed her on her back. The wild dark mane fell away, revealing a thin face, hollowed by suffering. Dark circles were imprinted beneath the closed eyes and the woman's lips were so dry and cracked that a trickle of blood ran down her chin. "Do you know her?"

"Don't you recognize her?"

There was something vaguely familiar about the woman's face, but Bruno couldn't place it. "Do you?"

"Yes." Jake reached out and began to gently stroke the woman's hair. "Mary . . ."

• • •

Blue eyes, keen eyes. Eyes she remembered from a long time ago, too long ago.

"It's all right, Mary. You're safe now, luv."

A man's husky voice, cockney accent. She knew that voice, too, but she had to search her memory through the mists of fog surrounding her. "Jake?"

"Right." His hand closed over her own on the coverlet. "You're going to be fine. You were badly dehydrated and you've been hooked up to an IV since last night, but the doctor says—"

"Doctor!" Memory came flooding back to her, and panic with it. She sat bolt upright in bed, her eyes wide with fear. "You shouldn't have called the doctor. He'll report it to Pallal. You shouldn't—"

"Easy." Jake's voice was soothing. "There'll be no report. Carlo's a friend of mine, and he doesn't like Pallal or his cronies any more than I do. I've called on him for help before."

"How long have I been here?"

"Since last night."

She looked down at herself and found she was wearing something green and silky. How long had it been since she'd worn anything but cotton prison garb? Her glance lifted and traveled around the small room. The furnishings were pleasant but not abundant—the bed on which she was lying, a Karastan carpet spilling across the white-stone floor, a Chinese lacquered cabinet occupying the space beside the long, narrow, recessed window. "Where are we?"

"At the house of my friend, Hassan Dalmar. He used to work for me. This room's above his cafe in the Casbah in Tarbol. You don't have to worry. You're safe here. The police leave the people of the

Casbah alone. It's not worth the risk to come into this part of town."

She knew that was true. Though she had lived on the affluent upper bank across the bay, she had heard for years that the twisting, crime-ridden streets of the Casbah held a thousand secrets. But he was wrong—she wasn't safe. She'd never be safe until—

She swung her legs to the floor. "Where are my clothes? I can't stay here. There's something I have to do."

Jake moved quickly forward. "For God's sake, you're still hooked up to the IV. Get back on the bed. You're not going anywhere."

She fumbled at the tube in her arm. "I'm fine. I don't have time for this. I have to—"

"You're not going anywhere." Jake grasped her shoulders and gazed down at her. "Not if I have to tie you down. Do you understand?"

His intensity was almost mesmerizing. She hesitated and then slowly lay back down on the pillows.

He tucked the covers carefully around her. Strange: His face held no expression, but his hands were trembling. He sat back down in the chair beside the bed. "I have a few questions and then I'll let you rest. Okay?"

She nodded warily.

"Do you know who I am?"

She nodded again.

"You . . . were dead." His voice was halting. "You and your father were supposed to have been killed in a private plane crash in the desert three years ago. When you didn't come to my apartment the next day, I went to yours. The servants said you'd left Said Ababa on a buying trip with your father.

That night there was a news bulletin on television saying the burned wreckage of the Harland company plane had been found." He paused. "You might say it was a bad time for me."

"It was a bad time for me, too," Mary said without inflection. "I arrived at Balahar that night."

"For God's sake, what happened?"

"Pallal. He wanted something from my father and Daddy wouldn't give it to him. Pallal killed him. He was already dead when you brought me home that evening. Pallal had been searching the house and . . ." She shook her head. "I was in the way."

"So he sent you to Balahar and staged the crash to protect himself." Jake closed his eyes. "And you've been there for three years?"

He seemed genuinely upset, she thought remotely. She would have believed a man of his background would have been more calloused.

Jake's eyes opened. "There are stories about Balahar." He said huskily, "Did they hurt you, Mary?"

"Torture me?" She shook her head. "No. I was kept in complete isolation. Sometimes I saw only the guards for months at a time. They didn't rape me, they didn't torture me; they just penned me up and forgot about me." She shivered. "Everybody in the world forgot about me."

"I didn't *know*, Mary." His eyes glittered in the lamplight. "As God is my witness, I thought you were dead."

"Sometimes I wished I were dead," Mary said dully. "It was like living in a vacuum. At first, I tried to remember what life was like outside, but that hurt too much. It was better not to think, not to remember—"

She broke off and her gaze lifted to his face. "There's no use talking about it. You wouldn't understand."

"I want to understand. I want to hear it all."

"Why?" Her lips curved in a bittersweet smile. "Because we spent eight hours together and you took my virginity? That was a lifetime ago for both of us. You don't have to pretend concern."

"Pretend? I'm not pretending, Mary."

Mary felt a faint stirring of emotion as she gazed at him. It felt . . . odd. "Then I thank you, but I have no need for sympathy. All I need is your help. I have something I must do, then I'll have to leave Said Ababa very quickly."

"And what do you have to do?"

Mary met his gaze steadily. "That's my affair. Will you take me away from here when it's time?"

He was silent a moment. "Yes." He stood up and moved toward the beaded door across the room. "We'll be leaving tonight, as soon as we can make arrangements."

"No, I told you—"

"I'm getting you out of Said Ababa now." Jake's tone was threaded with steel. "If you decide you can entrust this mysterious business to me, I'll be happy to help you, but I'm not letting you stay here in danger."

"It's my choice."

Jake shook his head. "No way. I'm not losing you again, luv. Now, get some sleep. I'll have Bruno bring you something to eat when you wake up." His lips twisted. "Remember the lobster dinner Bruno ordered for us? We never did get around to eating it."

"Didn't we?" She lowered her gaze to the sheet. "I . . . no, I'm sorry, I don't remember."

"The hell you don't." Jake's hands clenched into fists at his sides. "Mary, why—" He stood there looking at her for a moment and then shook his head. "I'll come and see you later." He pushed the beaded curtain aside and left the room.

Mary drew a deep, quivering breath and sat up in bed. She hadn't expected to feel this sudden aching sense of pain and loss. Jake Darcy meant nothing to her any longer. She had banished the memories of him during the hideous years in Balahar. Memories of the past only made the present harder to bear, and heaven knew, she mustn't let herself feel anything right now. If she started to feel again, she might shatter into a million pieces. That must not happen. Too much depended on her being in control.

She reached over and pulled the needle of the IV out of her arm, barely conscious of the sharp pain. She swung her feet to the floor and stood up.

Waves of dizziness assaulted her. She clutched desperately at the headboard of the bed, fighting to stay upright. When the whirling blackness passed, she looked around the room. Besides the beaded door through which Jake had left there was another on the other side of the room. She moved slowly, carefully, across the room toward the door. It opened to reveal a flight of spiraling stone steps leading to the street below.

Breathing a sigh of relief, she re-closed the door. She wasn't up to confronting Jake again this soon.

Now to find her clothes and get out.

"You look like hell," Bruno said bluntly as Jake sat down opposite him at the table in the cafe. He pushed the bottle of brandy and a glass across the table. "Have a drink."

"An excellent idea." Jake poured a generous quantity into the glass. "I feel like I've been run over by a truck."

"How is she?"

"Awake."

"And?"

"Not good." Jake tossed down the drink in two swallows. "I think I may kill Pallal. Would you care to help?"

"It seems an eminently worthwhile goal." Bruno's eyes searched Jake's face. "What did they do to her?"

"I don't know. She said they didn't torture her, but she's not the same. She's not *alive*." Jake's hand clenched the glass. "She glowed, Bruno. It was as if there was a light inside her, a gentle light—"

"You can't expect her to be the same."

"No, but I—Bruno, she's so damn wary of me."

"You're going to take her with us when we leave Said Ababa?"

"Of course I'm taking her. Did you think I was going to send her back to Balahar?"

"No." Bruno looked at the amber liquid in his glass. "Did it occur to you that her showing up in front of your Jeep after all these years was a little too much of a coincidence?"

Jake didn't answer.

"And that this particular timing when you're about to leave Said Ababa and Pallal—"

"It occurred to me," Jake said harshly. "I'm not blind, Bruno. She couldn't have escaped Balahar unless Pallal wanted her to escape." He poured another drink. "Or it could be that she didn't escape at all. Pallal could be forcing her to play the spy and phone him information as to where and when I'm leaving Said Ababa."

"And you're still willing to take her with us?"

Jake exploded. "Can you imagine what he might have done to Mary to force her to do what he wanted?" "She's a victim, dammit."

"And perhaps your enemy," Bruno said quietly. "What do you want me to do about her?"

Jake shook his head. "Nothing. I don't want her hurt, Bruno. She's been hurt enough. We'll just watch and wait. Set up another hiding place, in case we need to get out of here fast. She'll make a move toward Pallal if she's his agent."

"I'll put a tail on her." Bruno rose to his feet. "Chen?"

"I don't care." Jake lifted the glass to his lips. "Anyone. But do it right away. She's edgy and not going to wait long to make her move."

"Right away." Bruno raised his massive bulk out of the chair and moved toward the entrance of the cafe. "Don't kill that bottle. You may need all your wits about you."

Jake looked down into the depths of the brandy in his glass. "I know."

It was the noise that was so frightening, Mary thought as she hurried down the twisting streets back toward Hassan's cafe.

The shrill hawking of the vendors in the stalls

lining the streets, the loud bargaining, the rattle of the wheels of the pushcarts on the cobblestones.

The noise and the people pressing against her, smothering her. So many people. After years of solitary confinement in a tiny cell, she felt brutally assaulted by the noise. Her heart was beating so hard she could scarcely breathe. Only a few blocks more and she'd be free of them. She'd be back in the cafe, back in that quiet room, back with Jake.

Jake? Where had the thought come from? Jake was no sanctuary. Jake was from the past, and she could not rely on anyone but herself in this new world.

The sign for the cafe was just ahead. She was almost running now, her gaze fixed desperately on the winding stairs leading to the door on the upper floor. Just a few yards and she could close herself in for a little while and regain her strength and composure.

She darted up the steps, threw open the door and ran into the room. She leaned back against the door, breathing hard. She hadn't thought it would be this difficult. How was she to cope with the task ahead if she couldn't even go a few blocks without panicking?

She would be all right. On her first day of freedom it was to be expected she'd react with disorientation. She *had* to be all right.

She moved to the bed and sat down on it, trying to relax her tense muscles. The phone call had been made and now she had only to wait for the right moment.

．　　．　　．

"She's back upstairs. She went three blocks to another cafe and made a telephone call," Bruno said quietly. "Chen said he couldn't get close enough to hear the conversation but it took only three minutes." His lips twisted. "A little short if she just wanted to tell a friend the good news that she was alive and well."

Jake went still. "Lord, I hoped she wouldn't do it." He sat there, trying to think through the haze of pain enveloping him. She'd betrayed him. Mary had betrayed him.

"She probably told Pallal that she'd made contact and there was nothing concrete to report." Jake pushed back his chair and stood up. "We don't want Hassan endangered. We'll leave the cafe and take her to the casino. Send for the car."

"Jake, let her go. Leave her here." Bruno's voice was gentle. "You're too involved with her, and you're not thinking straight. She could get you killed or stuck in Balahar."

"I can't let her go."

"Then get her into the sack," Bruno said bluntly. "And stay there until she's out of your system. You've been thinking about her for three years and you've made her into some kind of dream woman. Turn her into reality."

"She is real to me." Jake left the cafe and climbed the outside stairs to the second-floor room.

Mary was lying on the bed, her eyes closed but her every muscle rigid, when he walked into the room. Her lids flew open and she gazed at him warily. He felt a jolt of aching sadness mix with the anger and frustration he was experiencing.

"We're leaving." He moved forward to stand beside the bed.

Her expression remained guarded as she scrambled to a sitting position.

"I assume you know why."

"You had me followed." It was a statement, not a question.

"Who did you call?"

She didn't answer.

"Pallal?" He hadn't really expected a reply and received none. "I won't compromise the safety of my friends. I'm moving you to my apartment over the casino a few miles from here." He grasped her wrist and pulled her to her feet.

She swayed and would have fallen if he hadn't caught her. He could feel the soft womanliness of her lower body against him and he hardened as if she had stroked him.

She looked up, startled, and met his gaze.

"What did you expect?" he asked thickly. "Isn't this what Pallal was counting on? He's not a man who believes in the more tender emotions, but he knows the power of sex." His hand caressed her throat and he felt the leap of her pulse beneath the sensitive tips of his fingers. "And so do you, don't you, luv? You knew how much you could move me, but you made a mistake in not realizing you'd be affected too." He looked down at her breasts, lifting and falling with the quickness of her breathing. "Any attraction that's so strong always goes two ways, Mary."

"Are we leaving?" she asked quietly. "Or do you want to have me first."

He smiled mockingly. "What would you do if I said yes?"

"Take off my clothes and lie down."

He stiffened and involuntarily stepped back.

She gazed at him levelly. "I have to stay with you, Jake, and you have to take me with you when you leave Said Ababa. I'll accomplish that any way I can."

He gazed at her a long moment. "Then I'd be a fool not to take advantage of the situation, wouldn't I?" He turned and grasped her arm. "But you'll forgive me if I refuse your invitation for the present. That IV hanging beside the bed would be bound to dampen my ardor a bit. I think I'll wait until you're in better shape for the sport."

"I thought you said we were going to leave Said Ababa tonight?"

"I've changed my mind." He propelled her toward the beaded curtain. "After your phone call I wouldn't want Pallal to have it too easy. You don't mind if we stay here a few days?"

"No." For an instant he saw the faintest flicker of relief before her face became shuttered. "I don't mind. Anything you want."

"Anything I want?" Jake's hand slipped down to pat her bottom. "What an interesting phrase, and what a truly magnanimous woman you're turning out to be." His hand suddenly grasped her arm and whirled her to face him. The mockery was completely gone from his expression. "Don't do this to me, Mary."

She stood looking at him without speaking.

"I'm not a bloody saint," he said with hoarse desperation. "I'm trying to understand but I'm raw inside. I feel betrayed, and my first instinct when I'm hurt is to hurt back. Give me something or someone else to fight and I'll do it."

She hesitated and then slowly shook her head. "I . . . can't."

The desperation faded from his face, to be replaced again by self-mockery. "Then I suppose I'll just have to take advantage of what perks there are for me in this situation, won't I?"

The casino was a small, two-story, stucco structure located on one of the back streets of the Casbah. Its only embellishment was an elaborately and beautifully carved mahogany door.

"It's not what I'd expect one of your casinos to look like," Mary said as she entered the small, dust-covered room. Slot machines, card tables and roulette wheels were draped with white sheets. Then she noticed the mirrors. She felt as if she were standing in the center of a box of mirrors. Mirrors covered the ceiling and every inch of the walls, mirrors so intricately cut they showed her reflection over and over. Even the bar against the far wall was mirrored. The only other decoration was the ornate ceiling fan that added a touch of *Casablanca* ambience to the club.

"I've always equipped and decorated my casinos to fit the environment." Jake pocketed the key with which he'd opened the door. "This one serves the inhabitants of the Casbah. A more glitzy place would intimidate them. I'm going to sign the deed over to Hassan when I'm safely out of the country, but right now it would be no gift. Everything and everyone connected with me is in danger."

"Is that why you're leaving Said Ababa?"

He shook his head. "I told you once I intended to turn totally legitimate within five years. I'm just a little ahead of schedule." He turned to Bruno, who had just come in from parking the car. "Mary will need some clothes. Do you suppose you can scare some up for her?"

"If she doesn't mind looking like something out of the *Arabian Nights*. Western clothes aren't very plentiful in the stalls of the Casbah." Bruno's face was expressionless, but Mary could sense his underlying hostility.

"I don't care what I wear." Mary moved toward a flight of blue and green mosaic-tiled stairs. "Is the apartment up here?"

Jake nodded and smiled sardonically. "Sorry, there's no back door."

"Well, the one at the cafe didn't do me much good, did it?" As she started to climb the stairs she heard the door close behind Bruno and then the click of Jake's steps on the mosaic tiles. Jake unlocked the door at the top of the stairs and stepped aside for her to precede him.

"One bedroom, one bath, a living room and kitchen combination," Jake enumerated as he closed the door and leaned against it. "Not fancy, but it will have to do. The electricity isn't even hooked up. You'd have been more comfortable at Hassan's. Too bad you blew it."

"This will be fine." She moved to the casement window and opened it to look out.

A back alley twisted down the hillside.

Jake suddenly stood behind her. "At least a twenty-foot jump. You'd have to knot some sheets together."

"I just wanted to get some air." She was surprised by the bitterness in his voice, and even more surprised that his tone hurt her. She'd thought her emotions would remain numb, but they were coming alive as rapidly as the sexuality that she'd become so abruptly aware of a short time ago.

She could feel the heat of Jake's body surrounding her and smell the clean spicy scent of his cologne. She felt her breasts swell in response. Her reaction to him now was as unthinking as it had been three years ago. Had Pallal been depending on her reaction, as he had been on Jake's?

She edged away from him. "Is that the bedroom?"

He gazed at her face. "One bed," he said deliberately.

She felt her pulse leap but kept her expression impassive. "Where will Bruno sleep?"

"He has a woman in the Casbah who'll be glad to put him up."

She moved toward the door he had indicated. "Then who'll protect you?"

"Against you?"

The hurt came again. "No, I think we're well enough matched. But you once told me you had many enemies."

"We're very well matched. You fit me like a glove. A very tight glove."

She hesitated at the door as the erotic picture his words generated caused a wave of heat to sear through her. He had said his first instinct when hurt was to strike back, and he was doing it, using a weapon he knew would be effective.

She opened the door to the bedroom, which was small and sparsely furnished with only a double bed, nightstand and bureau.

"No window." Jake stood leaning against the door-jamb. "And none in the bathroom either."

"I won't miss them." She moved toward the bed and kicked off her shoes. "I didn't have a window in my cell." She lay down on the bed and closed her eyes. "If you don't mind, I'd like to take a nap now. I'm very tired." She could feel his gaze on her from across the room and felt a tightening in her chest. "Do you suppose I could take a shower and shampoo my hair when I wake up?"

"That doesn't seem an exorbitant demand."

"It seems like one to me." She turned on her side. "I was only allowed to shower and wash my hair once a month at Balahar."

She heard him mutter something under his breath, and then the door slammed behind him.

He was gone. Mary's muscles gradually relaxed and she began to breathe easily again. A few minutes later she was deeply asleep.

"Time for dinner."

Mary opened her eyes to see Jake set a tray on the table beside her. She hurriedly sat up and brushed the hair from her face.

"By candlelight yet." He nodded at the four candles burning in the candelabra on the nightstand. "I wish I could claim it was my romantic soul, but the electricity isn't connected."

"I remember you said something about it being off." The room was in darkness except for the glowing flames of the candles. "How long did I sleep?"

"About nine hours." Jake sat down on the bed

beside her and uncovered the tray. "Your little jaunt exhausted you."

"Yes." She took the bowl and spoon Jake handed her. "What is it?"

"Lamb stew. It's pretty good. I made it myself."

It was good. Light and creamy and flavored with herbs. She ate silently and hungrily for a few moments. "You cook?"

"I'm a man of many talents. I only had time to show you one of them during our previous acquaintance."

She kept her gaze lowered to the contents of her bowl. "Where did you learn to cook?"

"In Queensland."

"Australia? Is there any place you haven't been?"

"Not many." He pushed a strand of hair back from her face.

Her hand stopped with the spoon halfway to her mouth. The very casualness of the action was almost unbearably intimate. She lifted the spoon to her lips. "I've only been to the United States and Great Britain."

"Then your experience has been limited. Everyone should see Australia. It's like being on another planet." He looked down at the bowl. "You were hungry. More?"

"No, thank you."

He started to smile. "You always were a polite little girl." His smile faded as he picked up the napkin, patted her lips as if she were a small child, then tossed it carelessly back on the tray. "But you're not a little girl any longer, are you?" He took the spoon and bowl and set them on the tray before standing up. "Bath time. No shower stall, but the bathtub's king-size and Bruno found some English shampoo at one of the stalls where he bought those." He gestured at the shimmering pile of material on the chair across the room and two pairs of silk slippers on the floor beside the chair. "There's a hairbrush on the bureau. Why don't you tackle those tangles while I run your bath?"

Before she could reply he was gone, and a moment later she heard the sound of running water. She threw back the covers and padded to the pile of clothes on the chair. Two caftans, both with square low necks, one fashioned in emerald green brocade, the other in a vibrant aqua silk. No underthings. Well, at least it wasn't harem pajamas, she thought.

She picked up the aqua caftan and found the hairbrush on the bureau. She sat down on the bed with her legs crossed tailor fashion and began the painful process of removing the tangles.

"Ready?" Jake stood in the bathroom doorway.

"As much as I can be." She made a face. "These blasted tangles won't come out."

"I'll work them out when I have the shampoo on."

She looked at him warily. "You?"

"Why are you surprised?" He smiled mockingly. "We're hardly strangers. I've even helped you bathe before." His smile faded. "I want to *see* you."

She stood up and tossed the brush and gown onto the chair. "You're right; I don't know why I was startled." She pulled the tunic over her head and threw it aside. "It doesn't matter." In another moment she was completely nude and stood before him passively. "Shall I turn around for your complete inspection?"

He stood stiff, every muscle tense as his gaze went slowly over her. "That won't be necessary."

"I thought you'd be disappointed. I'm skin and bones." She carefully kept her voice casual. His gaze on her body was igniting tiny hot explosions between her thighs, at the tips of her breasts, even on the soles of her feet.

"I'm not disappointed. You're too thin, but your breasts are fuller . . ." His gaze moved down to the curls that encircled her womanhood and she felt a sudden jolt of heat. "You're beautiful."

"Nonsense." She moved toward the bathroom. "I'm not at all beautiful. I never was."

The tub was the same blue and green mosaic as the steps and it was filled with bubbles. She sank down into the hot water with a sigh of contentment and closed her eyes. "Wonderful."

"You're not at all shy about displaying your body."

She opened her eyes to see Jake standing in the doorway, rolling up the sleeves of his black shirt.

"Or was that to show me how little I disturb you these days?"

"Did you expect modesty?" She looked at him calmly. "The guards saw me naked every time I showered. They weren't allowed to touch but they weren't forbidden to look. I became accustomed to men's eyes on me." She started rubbing shampoo into her hair.

He knelt behind her and began to knead the scalp, his fingers deftly threading through the tangles. His voice was hoarse. "You shouldn't have told me that."

"Why not? It's the truth."

"Because it makes me mad as hell." His tone was

raw and intense. "I never thought I was a particularly possessive bloke. . . . I should feel sorry for you, right?"

"I don't want sympathy."

"Dip your head."

She dipped her head beneath the stream of water and he rinsed the soapsuds from it.

"I don't feel sorry for you. I want to kill the men who were looking at you and I want to . . ." His hands moved from her hair to cup her breasts beneath the water. "I want them to see me touch you like this." His lips moved to her nape as his hands slowly squeezed and released her, then squeezed again. "I want them to know that it's only for me."

The muscles of her stomach clenched as fire streaked through her.

His teeth closed on her right earlobe. She shivered, biting her lips to stifle a cry.

"Lord, I've missed you, Mary," he whispered.

He meant he had missed her body, she thought. How could he have missed anything else about her when he hadn't really known her? Yet his voice held such sincerity she could almost believe him.

"Say something," he said hoarsely.

"I don't know what you want me to say." Her voice was shaking. "You do arouse me. You can see that you do."

His hands stilled on her breasts. "Lord, I don't want—" He stopped, and when he spoke again his voice was once more layered with mockery. "Am I to assume that means you give your heartfelt assent?"

"I told you I'd do anything you asked."

"You did, didn't you?" He stood up and put his hands beneath her arms and lifted her from the tub. "Not that I'd forgotten." He began to dry her with the rough terry towel. "It's not the kind of offer that slips a man's mind." He handed her another towel. "Go dry your hair."

She looked at him uncertainly and then took the towel and left the bathroom.

She heard him empty the tub and then begin to clean it. She would have thought he'd send for someone to do that homely task. He was obviously a rich man now. But he had cooked her meal and now was scrubbing the bathtub. Curious.

Her body tingled and there was a heavy ripeness to the breasts he had held in his hands. She sat down on the bed and began to towel dry her hair, purposely blocking out all thought. She had become very good at that in the last three years.

She was running a comb through her still-damp hair when he came back into the bedroom.

He stopped. "You didn't put your clothes on."

"You didn't tell me to dress," she said quietly. "I thought it might be a waste of time."

He picked up the aqua caftan and strode across the room. "Stand up."

He sounded angry. She slowly put down her comb and rose to her feet. He tugged the silk caftan over her head; it billowed around her.

"Lord." His gaze was on the low square neckline, which just covered her nipples, leaving the upper breasts to swell from their silken confinement.

"Bruno seems to be something of a voyeur," she said calmly. "Or did he think you'd like this?"

"Oh, he knew I'd like it." Jake smiled sardonically, his gaze never leaving her breasts. "He wants me to make love to you."

"Really? I got the distinct impression he resented me."

"He does. Bruno has absolute loyalty and he can't stand disloyalty in others."

She flinched. The words shouldn't have hurt her, but they did. "Then why?"

"He thinks if I jump your bones, it will be over." His head was slowly lowering. "He wants me to get you out of my system."

She could barely breathe; his warm breath seared her skin as his lips hovered over her breasts. His warm lips touched first one breast and then the other. "You'd really sleep with me. Do anything I ask, wouldn't you?"

"Yes." She closed her eyes and let the heat move through her. She felt the hard line of his cheek resting against her bare, soft breast.

"What did he do to you?"

Suddenly his cheek was gone and his hands dug into her shoulders. Her lids flew open.

He shook her. "What the hell did he do to you to make you like this?"

His face above her was twisted, tormented, and she suddenly wanted desperately to stop his pain. She opened her lips to speak and then closed them again.

She swallowed. "I have to stay with you and you have to take me with you."

"You said that before. Dammit, you sound like you've been brainwashed. Is that what happened?"

"No, not in the way you mean." She looked up at him. "Shall I get into bed?"

He stared at her for a long moment before releasing her. "Yes, go to bed."

She felt his gaze on the middle of her back as she moved toward the bed and pulled back the coverlet.

The door slammed and she looked over her shoulder in startled alarm.

Jake was gone.

Four

"I think we've definitely got to get you something else to wear." Jake's gaze lingered on the exposed flesh swelling from the bosom of the green brocade caftan before turning back to the stove. "Did you sleep well?"

"Yes." She sat down at the table and watched him expertly flip a pancake. "You do that like a professional."

"I was the cook at the officers' club in Sydney. One of my more respectable occupations." He scooped the pancake onto a plate with two others and set them before her. "The bacon's on the plate under that napkin. Eat."

"You always seem to be feeding me."

"You need food." He went to the refrigerator and got out a carton of milk. "Your hair looks nice."

"It's terrible. All split ends."

He walked over and poured milk into her glass. "I like it. It's practically down to your waist now." He picked up a long strand and rubbed it between his thumb and forefinger, enjoying the textures. "I remember it being so much shorter than this . . ."

She stopped eating and sat looking up at him.

He dropped the strand. "No, I'm not going to drag you into the bedroom and rape you," he said roughly. "But that's right, it wouldn't be rape. You'd be more than willing." He sat down on the chair opposite her. "I once knew a girl in a house in Bangkok like you."

"Did you?" She continued to eat.

"No." His hands slowly clenched into fists. "That's a lie. I've never known anyone like you."

"Aren't you going to eat?"

"I ate earlier." He extended his legs out in front of him and gazed at her moodily. "I don't know what the hell I'm going to do with you."

"I thought you'd already decided." She sipped the milk, her eyes lowered. "I was surprised when you left last night."

"So was I." He glanced down at her plate. "You've barely touched your food."

"It's too much. My stomach must have shrunk." She added quickly, "But it was very good. Thank you."

For an instant an amused grin lighted up his face. "You're very welcome." His smile faded. "I can't figure you out and it's driving me bats, luv. You've got to help me."

She finished her milk. "What do you want me to do?"

"I have to get to know you again." He looked down at the floor, frowning. "Mah-jongg."

She blinked. "What?"

"Mah-jongg. Do you know how to play it?"

She looked at him in bewilderment. "No."

"Well, you're about to learn." He stood up. "I'll wash the dishes and be right with you. Go into the living room and wait for me."

"You've been doing everything. I can wash the dishes."

He shook his head. "I like doing things for you. I didn't think I'd ever again have the chance. . . ."

She felt a strange, sweet pang as she watched him move about the kitchen. She mustn't feel like this, she thought. It was all right if she felt desire. The very mindlessness of lust kept her safe, but she mustn't become emotionally involved with Jake.

Desire. She willed herself to think only of his physical presence. He moved with smooth, economical definition, every action purposeful. His strong thighs and tight buttocks, outlined by the sun-faded softness of his jeans, were magnificent. His entire body was exceptional, she remembered. Compact, powerful, yet with a virile grace that aroused and fascinated. The memory brought a hot tingling, the familiar breathlessness, blocking out the dangerous feeling of tenderness.

She stood up and moved toward the living room. "I'll see if my pants and tunic are dry. I rinsed them out and hung them on the windowsill."

"Do that." He shot her a grin over his shoulder as he turned on the faucets at the sink. "Mah-jongg requires a certain amount of concentration. I don't want to give myself too much of a handicap. It's humiliating being beaten by an amateur at the game."

"I like chess better," Mary said as she looked down

at the mah-jongg board on the coffee table. "I used to play chess with my father."

"We'll play chess next time. I thought learning something new would distract you."

"So that you could get to know how I think?" Mary's gaze lifted to meet his. "Did you succeed?"

He nodded slowly. "I learned you're cautious, intelligent, and honest."

"All from four hours of playing mah-jongg?"

"You can learn a lot about people from games of chance. Come to one of my casinos sometime and watch the players. I think you'd find it interesting. Did you discover anything about me?"

"You didn't let me win. That means you respect the spirit of the game and your opponent."

"Would you have liked me to let you win?"

"No, I would have hated it."

"Excellent. See how much progress we're making?" He sat back in his chair. "Now come over here."

She stiffened in surprise.

"Four hours of play is enough; I'm not a cerebral man," he said softly. "And you didn't change out of that caftan."

"My clothes weren't dry."

"I'm not complaining. Come here."

She slowly rose from the couch, came around the coffee table, and stood before his easy chair. His position in the chair was indolent, yet she could feel his tension. Or was it her own? Her knees felt so weak she had to stand very stiff to keep from falling.

"Such pretty hair." He reached up and pulled two long tresses forward and arranged them to half-veil her breasts. "Come down to me, luv." He pulled her onto his lap and held her close, rocking her back and forth while his fingers tangled in her hair. "Such a pretty Mary."

Tender cosseting and stark arousal. How could the two exist side by side, Mary wondered. Yet there was no doubt they did here in Jake's embrace. His chest was rising and falling with the harshness of his breathing; the flesh of his throat felt hot against her cheek.

He slipped the neckline of the caftan down, pressing his lips to the exact spot where her shoulder joined her upper arm. "You like being here? You like me holding you?"

"Yes." She swallowed to ease the tightness of her throat.

"Then show me, luv." He lifted her and sat her astraddle him with both knees on the cushioned seat of the chair. He tugged gently at her long hair. "Kiss me."

She leaned slowly toward him, feeling the hard maleness of him pressing against her womanhood, smelling the spicy cleanness surrounding him, the heat of his chest through the layers of clothes separating them. His lips were slightly parted and she could see the blue of his eyes glittering from beneath half-closed lids as she drew closer and closer.

He sat perfectly still, letting her do it all.

Her lips touched his gently, tentatively, and he didn't move.

Then his mouth opened and his tongue invaded her lazily, sensuously, intimately. He groaned with pleasure low in his throat, and the sound sent another tingling thrill of arousal through her.

Now his lips were moving, one hand shifting her

head to please himself in a dozen positions while the other hand pushed the caftan down about her hips.

"Open my shirt," he muttered between kisses. "Hurry. I want to feel you against me."

Her hands trembled on the buttons and finally managed to part his shirt. His chest was laboring, the thick, dark triangle of hair there superbly male.

He jerked her to him.

She shivered at the hot shock of his hard flesh against her sensitive nipples. His hands moved caressingly down her smooth back as he rubbed her against the springy wiriness of the thatch of hair on his chest, an erotic brand burning her. She could hear herself making soft little cries as his lips took and took and his body gave and gave. . . .

"Sweet baby. My baby." His voice was shaking as he pulled the caftan up so that there was nothing between them but his clothing. "You want it. You want me. Right, luv? It's like before."

He was warm and hard and still inaccessible, she realized in frustration. She rubbed against him frantically, she pressed closer, her back arching, her head thrown back. "Jake."

"Say it." His lips pressed against her throat. "I have to hear you say it. It's like before—"

"Anything you want," she whispered.

She could feel him stiffening against her.

"Anything I want," he repeated. "But not because—" He lifted her off him with scarcely restrained violence.

"Good Lord, anything I want." He laughed mirthlessly as he jerkily stood up and turned away. "Well, heaven knows I want you. I want it so bad, it's damn well ripping my guts out."

"I . . . I don't understand." She slowly pulled the caftan back onto her shoulders. "Why are you angry?"

"Because I do understand. When you came to me you intended to sleep with me no matter how you felt about me, didn't you?"

"If necessary." She saw him flinch and went on quickly, "You say you understand, but you don't. You don't understand anything."

"Then *help* me." His gaze moved slowly over her. "But tell me one thing. Did Pallal order you to sleep with me?"

She hesitated. "Yes, but I—"

"That's enough." He held up his hand and smiled with an effort. "I knew it anyway, but I just had to hear you put it in words." He started to button his shirt. "And do you know something? Once I get used to the idea, I'll probably let you do your duty. I want you that much." He started toward the door. "But you'll excuse me if I pass right now. I'm feeling a little raw."

The door slammed behind him and she heard the sound of a key turning in the lock, then his footsteps on the mosaic tile of the steps.

She stood there in the middle of the room gazing at the closed door. Her body still ached with arousal and some part of her ached because of the pain she had just seen in Jake's expression. She hadn't wanted to hurt him. She didn't want to hurt anyone. Why did life have to be like this?

Jake didn't return until early afternoon.

Mary straightened when she heard his key in the lock, her fingers biting into the cushioned arms of the easy chair.

"You've been gone a long time," she said as he walked into the room.

"Am I to assume you missed me?" Jake's tone was sardonic as he closed the door behind him. "It took a little time for me to feel able to face you again. I had to cool off in more ways than one."

"You locked the door."

"In the state I was in, I didn't want to be forced to chase after you." His smile was twisted. "All my primitive instincts were aroused to fever pitch. I would have brought you down."

"I wasn't complaining. I'm used to being locked up."

He flinched. "Low blow, Mary."

"It's the truth." Mary rose and smoothed the caftan around her. "But I hated being your prisoner. It was different somehow." She gazed at him directly. "You're not being sensible. There was no reason for you to be so angry. I wasn't even fighting you."

"That was why I was angry. And who says I have to be sensible? I seem to be operating on a purely emotional level where you're concerned." He held out his hand. "Come here. We're going downstairs."

She looked at him, puzzled. "Downstairs? Why?"

"To the casino." He smiled bitterly. "Because I want you there. Didn't you say you'd do anything I wanted? You're not being very compliant."

She moved slowly across the room and put her hand in his.

He didn't flinch this time, but his lips tightened as if he were in pain as he looked down at her hand. "I wish you hadn't done that," he said thickly. His hand closed on hers with bruising strength. "But that's an irrational reaction, isn't it? I should be glad you're ready to obey my every command. I'd be stupid not to take advantage of the situation." He opened the door. "And I'm not stupid, Mary. Blind sometimes, but not stupid. So let's see just how far you'll go to get what you want." He turned, pulling her down the tiled stairs and only releasing her as they reached the bottom. "Wait here." He strode across the casino toward the mirrored bar across the room.

"Why are we here?" Mary looked around the sheet-draped tables in bewilderment. Afternoon sunlight poured through the arched windows fronting the street, forming a brilliant dappling on the shadowy tables, reflecting like spotlights off the mirrors on the far side of the room, and bouncing off the mirrors on the ceiling. She could see her own and Jake's reflections everywhere, repeated over and over in the mirrors that encircled the room.

"Because there's more room here than upstairs." Jake lifted a portable cassette deck from behind the bar, took a cassette from his pocket, and inserted it into the machine. "And I want to dance with you." He pressed the starter button. "You remember this tune?"

The bittersweet strains of "Softly, As I Leave You" wafted across the room. Memories rushed back to Mary in an evocative stream. The scent of flowers and white damask tablecloths, the gentle clink of china cups. Jake taking her into his arms and holding her with shocking intimacy.

As he was taking her in his arms now. He pushed her head down on his shoulder and began to move to the music. "I couldn't stand hearing that song for months after the plane crash," he said in a low voice. "Because you didn't leave me softly. It was as cruel and sharp as a stab in the heart. But after a while I found I wanted to listen to it. Not all the time—just when I felt lonely or lost."

"I can't imagine you ever feeling lost." The music was almost painfully nostalgic, Mary thought, moving closer to him. Yes, "painful" was the word. She found her throat aching and she swallowed to ease its tightness.

"I have my moments."

The music ended and then began to play again while they continued to move slowly. Mary caught glimpses of their reflections in the mirrors as they turned, and it was almost like being on a dance floor with other couples. The music ended and started again, and Mary knew she couldn't bear for it to go on much longer. The emotion binding them together had far different overtones now than it had before. Not sexual. Just poignantly, overpoweringly intimate. She unconsciously began to stiffen, resisting that intimacy.

"Loosen up." He lifted his head to look down at her and, when he saw her expression, his gaze narrowed. "This scares you, doesn't it? You don't like remembering that afternoon, that night. Why not?"

"It's in the past. It has no bearing on what we are now."

"The hell it doesn't. Every past experience makes us what we are now." His lips twisted. "Maybe you just don't like thinking of me as anything but the mark Pallal set up for you to take. Well, I'm human, I bleed. Do you want to know how badly I bled when I thought you were dead?"

She quickly looked down as she felt a wrenching pang of regret. "No."

"I didn't think you would. You have to keep yourself guarded, because you're afraid you won't be able to give Pallal what he wants if you get too close to me."

She was silent for a moment and then tried to change the subject. "We're only moving to the music. You still don't know how to dance."

"You remember? Don't you consider that dangerous to admit?" His tone had the dry sharpness of a razor on leather and she could feel the anger and frustration building in him again. "If you're not careful, I might actually think that night meant more to you than a pleasant roll in the hay." He stopped moving and looked down at her with a reckless smile. "But it was more than pleasant, wasn't it? It blew our minds. Perhaps that's what you need again to remind you who I am." His hand grasped her wrist and he pulled her toward the bar. "Heaven forbid sentiment should enter our relationship now."

"You're hurting my wrist."

"Consider yourself lucky. I feel like breaking your neck." He stopped before the cassette deck and turned off the music. "Get on the bar."

"It's too high."

His hands clasped her waist and lifted her so that she was sitting on the mirrored surface of the bar. He backed away from her and levered himself up on a baccarat table a few yards away. "Kick off your slippers."

She frowned in puzzlement, but a moment later the green satin slippers fell to the floor.

His gaze traveled over the bare feet peeping from beneath the hem of the caftan to the nakedness of her throat and upper breasts revealed by the low neckline of the gown.

"Erotic."

"Bare feet?" She laughed shakily. She could feel the tightly leashed anger and desire charging the atmosphere between them with waves of tension.

"Bare Mary." Jake's left foot swung lazily back and forth, belying the rigid message of his neck and shoulders. "The minute we walked into the casino I realized how this box of mirrors would suit you." His voice lowered to silken softness. "But no more than it would suit me. Take off the caftan, Mary."

She met his gaze across the yards separating them. His expression was hard and unrelenting, the face of the man she had glimpsed only for a moment those years ago when he'd been speaking to Pallal. The man Karen had described as mad, bad, dangerous to know.

"What are you waiting for?" He smiled faintly. "You said you'd do anything I asked. Nudity is nothing to you, remember? All of those damned prison guards."

"You didn't seem to want to see me unclothed last night."

"I still had hope last night. It rapidly faded away. Take off the caftan."

She drew a long shaky breath and knelt on the bar. With one graceful movement she pulled the caftan off and let it fall in a swath of brilliant emerald on the glittering mirrored surface of the bar.

She looked up and met Jake's eyes again. "This feels very strange. The mirrors . . ." She looked up at the mirror on the ceiling and saw her own naked form on the bar. Her glance traveled to the image of Jake, watching her intently. Everywhere she looked she could see them both, her own nudity and Jake's eyes . . . a multitude of images, all strangers and yet all Jake.

"Strange. But I think you like it." He gazed at her nipples, hardening under the stimulus of that barrage of images. "I thought you would. You look like am exquisite statue kneeling there with your hair all around you. Shake your head, hard."

She shook her head and could feel her hair swish about her shoulders, could feel the slight jounce of her breasts at the movement.

"That's better. Now, tell me how you feel."

She was silent a moment. "Vulnerable." She moistened her lips with her tongue. "Is this really necessary?"

The dozens of images of Jake nodded slowly. "It's what I want. Doesn't that make it necessary? I have to have what I want, don't I, luv? That's what this is all about. Give Jake what he wants, and he'll put his head right on the old chopping block." He jumped down from the table and strolled across the room toward her. She could feel herself tense as the dozens of images converged upon her until there was only one flesh-and-blood, three-dimensional Jake standing before her. She could see the rapid pulse in the hollow of his throat and the faint flush darkening his tanned cheeks. "Answer me. Isn't that what Pallal wants you to do, Mary?"

She sat there gazing at him, her hands closing into fists at her sides. It would be over soon, she told herself. The pain in Jake's face, her own helplessness. One way or another, it would be over soon.

"You're not answering me."

"I don't think you want an answer."

"Very perceptive." He took a step nearer. "I'm no masochist. I don't want to hear you say it again."

"Jake . . . it's not what you think. I don't want to hurt you."

He stopped, his gaze flying to her face. "My God, then *talk* to me."

She gazed at him helplessly, her eyes glittering with tears.

"Oh no, you don't do that to me again," Jake said harshly. "I don't mind letting you win, but I'll be damned if I let Pallal call the shots." He lowered his head and his lips closed on her nipple. She shuddered as fire shot through her and she instinctively arched toward him.

His hands moved slowly over her abdomen, stroking, petting her as he sucked strongly.

She cried out, her fingers tangling in his hair.

He lifted his head and an expression of intense pain crossed his face before he gazed fiercely into her eyes. "Pallal's not going to win, Mary."

He pushed her gently back on the glittering, mirrored surface of the bar and parted her legs. "He's not going to make a whore of you, because I'm not going to take what I want." She saw the reflections of his curly dark hair in the mirror on the ceiling lower, come toward her. The mirror was cold on her naked back but his hands were warm as he arranged her to suit himself. She bit her lower lip to keep from crying out as she felt his hard cheek against the softness of her inner thigh. "Instead, I'm going to give you what you want. I'm going to give and give until you scream with pleasure." She could feel his warm breath, and the muscles of her stomach clenched helplessly. "Don't you think that's an excellent plan? And maybe, if I'm lucky, you'll remember that night three years ago and realize why I can't let him do this to us." His warm tongue touched her.

He kept his promise.

Moments later Mary did scream with pleasure.

She felt distinctly shaky as Jake slipped the caftan back over her head and settled the folds around her. She was weak, lethargic, almost comatose from the pleasure Jake had given her, and yet she knew he was still completely unsatisfied. "I don't understand you."

"I know you don't." Jake found her slippers on the floor, lifted her left foot and put one of them on her. "Nothing could be clearer." He slipped the right slipper on and then lifted her off the bar onto her feet. "It might help you to know that I'm fighting for my life. No, *our* life. Otherwise those mirrors would have reflected a completely different but equally erotic picture." He looked down at her. "Though I enjoyed the hell out of this too. I like pleasing you, luv."

She gazed at him, troubled. "It doesn't change anything, Jake. I don't see why you did it." She shook her head and repeated, "I just don't understand you."

"Maybe I'm working toward spiking the tiniest break in the dam." He smiled mirthlessly. "Or maybe I'll have to rely on a cumulative effect." He led her toward the staircase. "Go on upstairs. I have to see Bruno and make a few arrangements."

She started up the stairs. She could feel his gaze on her back with every step, and as she reached the top she looked over her shoulder and found him still at the foot of the staircase, his gaze fixed on her with frustration and desperation.

"You'll be back soon?"

"In an hour or two. What do you want for dinner?"

"It doesn't matter."

"Then I'll improvise." He still stood there, as if reluctant to go. "Though I doubt if I could get lobster or chocolate ice cream on such short notice in this section of town."

Chocolate ice cream. We'll have it next time, he had said as he took her in his arms in the shower.

And three years later he still remembered that promise.

"I can wait," she said gently.

"Yeah." He stood looking at her for another moment before turning on his heel and moving toward the front entrance. "Another time."

The carved mahogany door slammed behind him.

She stood there looking at the elaborate floral carvings on the door for a few minutes before she realized she hadn't heard the key turn in the lock.

Had he forgotten?

Or was it a trap?

It didn't matter. She had no option but to grasp the opportunity as it presented itself. Time was running out. When would Jake decide to leave Said Ababa? She could sense his impatience and frustration growing with every passing moment.

She hurried into the apartment, went to the window, and checked the pants and tunic. Dry, except for the collar of the tunic. It would have to do. There was no telling when she'd get another chance to leave the apartment.

She picked up the clothes and carried them into the bedroom.

She would go first to the warehouse and then phone and arrange a meeting with Pallal.

• • •

"Pleasant night?" Bruno asked as Jake came behind the stall to stand beside him beneath the striped awning of the shop across from the casino. "You don't appear to be in a good temper."

"Lousy night. And equally lousy temper." Jake leaned back against the wall. "Hassan?"

"No raid on the cafe. But that doesn't mean it isn't watched." Bruno's gaze went to the window above the casino. "I thought the caftans would do the trick."

"You have an evil and devious mind, mate."

"It's from associating with the crude types you've exposed me to over the years." Bruno paused. "Do you think she's going to try to contact him again?"

"Probably. Pallal has her well and truly under his thumb," Jake said wearily. "He snaps his fingers, she jumps."

"So you're giving her another chance to put your head in the noose?"

"She doesn't know how or when we're leaving the country yet. She can't give him much."

"Who follows her?"

"I do. I don't want to take the chance of you 'losing' her beneath the wheels of a bus or in the river."

"Better her than you." Bruno's expression hardened. "I get quite annoyed with traitors."

"Lethally annoyed."

"Is there any other way?" He glanced soberly at Jake. "She's tying you up in knots. I've never seen you like this. Hell yes, I'd get rid of her any way I could. She's not important to me and you are."

"But she's important to me," Jake murmured. "God, help me. So I'll be the one to follow her."

"Well, it looks like you're going to get your chance."

Jake's gaze followed Bruno's to the ornately carved door across the street. The door had opened and Mary stood in the doorway. She stood there for a moment as the shouts and smells of the street assaulted her. Then, she squared her shoulders as if bracing herself, turned left, and walked quickly down the street.

Pallal didn't bother to stand up when she approached the table in the cafe where he was sitting. Mary didn't expect the courtesy. She had learned over the years of dealing with him that Rustin Pallal's rudeness was a calculated tool to point out both his position of power and her own helplessness.

"You may sit down." His gaze traveled over her objectively. "You look much better than when I last saw you. Have you fully recovered?"

"Yes." Mary sat down in the chair opposite him. She tried to keep her expression shuttered, but she could feel the nervous panic rising within her. After all these years of conditioning, to fear him was an automatic response. "I have nothing to report as yet."

His expression remained bland. "I expected more from you," he said. "You have no idea how he's to leave the country?"

"Not yet."

"But he will take you with him?" A bit of menace entered his tone.

"He says he will."

"That's not good enough. I thought I impressed on you the urgency of the matter. Jake Darcy must be persuaded to take you with him, and I must be informed how he's to leave the country." One black brow arched inquiringly. "Should I reinforce that urgency?"

"No," she said quickly. "I'll find out for you."

"Perhaps you haven't been persuasive enough. Have you slept with him yet?"

"There have been . . . intimacies."

Pallal's gaze narrowed on her face. "My sources say Darcy will be departing Said Ababa with at least five million dollars in liquid assets. I won't be cheated out of that money by your lack of cooperation, Mary."

"I am cooperating," she said desperately. "Haven't I done everything you told me to do?"

"I don't know. Have you?" He leaned back in his chair. "I'm not sure this way was best, after all. Perhaps I should return you to Balahar. I need only to raise my voice and you will be taken into custody."

"No!" It mustn't happen, she thought frantically. Not when she was so close. "I'll find out the information you want." She scrambled to her feet. "You haven't given me enough time."

He watched her with cool calculation. "Perhaps you're right. I do tend to get impatient when a great deal of money is involved. I'll allow you two more days. However, you'll call me both tonight and tomorrow night and report your progress."

"If I can," she said, almost limp with relief.

"Not if." Pallal smiled. "I dislike that word. Make it happen, Mary. Make it all happen." His smile vanished. "You know both the consequences and the rewards."

"Yes, I know." She moistened her lips with her tongue. "May I go now? I should be getting back."

He nodded. "By all means." He lifted his absinthe to his lips and sipped delicately. "We wouldn't want Darcy to become impatient for your company."

She hesitated. Should she take advantage of the opportunity?

No, Pallal always had guards about him. She was as helpless now as she had been at Balahar.

"You have something more to tell me?" Pallal asked.

"No, nothing more."

She turned and swiftly left the cafe.

Her breath was painful in her lungs as Mary went through the carved mahogany door, hurried up the mosaic-tile steps, and opened the door at the top of the staircase.

This time had been worse than the time before, she thought desperately. The noise. The honking of horns. The people. Would she ever get used to it?

She closed the door behind her, ran to the open window, and slammed it shut. That was better. She had closed out the clamor and noise, the pushing, thrusting crowds of people, for the moment. She pressed her forehead against the cool glass and tried to steady her breathing.

It was done.

She needn't face that horror again until she contacted Pallal. She could stay here and let the silence—

"Have a nice trip?"

She turned to see Jake standing in the doorway.

He closed the door behind him. "You're quite pale. I'm not sure I should let you go running about the city if you're going to injure yourself." He smiled bitterly. "Or try to injure me."

"I . . . don't like . . . crowds."

"You've been gone almost four hours." His expression didn't change. "Would you like to tell me where you've been?"

"No." Her heartbeat was steadying now. "I don't think I have to, do I?"

"Let me save you a few lies," Jake said wearily. "You went out of the Casbah and across town to a warehouse on the docks. You stayed there for ten minutes, made a telephone call, and then met Pallal thirty minutes later at a cafe near the warehouse."

"You had me followed?"

"I accorded myself that honor. Tell me, did you tell Pallal where I was, Mary?"

"No."

Jake crossed the room and grasped her shoulders with bruising strength. "For God's sake, tell me the truth. You don't have to be afraid of Pallal. I'll help you. I don't care if he set you on me."

"I *have* to be afraid of him. You don't know what he can do." Mary's eyes were suddenly blazing at him. "And you don't have to help me. I can help myself. I won't let Pallal win." She tore herself away from him. "Of course he set me on you. He planned to use me all along. Why do you think he didn't kill me right away? You made inquiries after the plane crash and that made him curious. He remembered you'd noticed me that night and sent someone to the apartment building who remembered about the dinner being sent up. He told me he'd considered killing me but that he'd reconsidered when he found out he might be holding something you might possibly want." She smiled mirthlessly. "In a way, I suppose you saved my life. Though after a year in that cell I wasn't sure I should be grateful."

"What did you tell Pallal today, Mary?"

She crossed her arms over her chest to try to stop their trembling. "Nothing. I won't let him win. Do you think I'd let him turn me into the monster he is? I knew what he'd do to you."

He took an impulsive step forward and then stopped as he saw her tense warily. "Why did you go to the warehouse?"

"I had to have a weapon to fight him. He wants you, but he wants the Princess more."

"The Princess?"

She fumbled in the pocket of her tunic and drew out a flat jeweler's case. "The Burgundy Princess. It's a twelve-carat teardrop ruby on a diamond chain. It's worth over a million dollars. My father worshiped it. The Princess was the pride of his collection." She shuddered. "That's why Pallal killed my father. He wanted the Princess. He'd been trying to coerce my father into giving it to him in exchange for an exit visa for the two of us, but Daddy refused. Pallal became impatient." She stopped and then forced herself to go on. "That night he tied him to a chair and had him beaten to try to force him into telling him where the necklace was hidden." Her eyes filled with tears. "But he went too far. He killed him. Accidentally."

"Lord," Jake whispered.

"Pallal has the Eastern view that women are chattels, and it never occurred to him Daddy would have told me where he had hidden it. He raided the safe-deposit boxes and Daddy's offices. He wasn't at all pleased when he didn't find what he wanted."

"You could have bargained with it for your freedom."

She shook her head. "Not while I was in Balahar under his thumb. I had to wait for a chance."

Jake's lips twisted. "Me?"

"I had to tell him I'd do it," she whispered. "It was my one hope. I had to get out of there and find the Princess to have ammunition with which to bargain with him. I was helpless and I couldn't stay that way."

"What did he promise you for my head? An exit visa from Said Ababa."

"More."

"Twenty pieces of silver?" Jake wearily shook his head. "I'm sorry. I didn't mean that. I know you were probably desperate."

"Yes, very desperate." She met his gaze steadily. "He promised me my son, Jake."

Five

Jake froze. "Your . . . son?"

Mary moved to the window and looked out blindly at the street below. "They let me keep him with me at first, for the first eight months, and then they took him away. Pallal said he was being cared for by a woman who lived in the village by the prison." She swallowed to ease the tightness of her throat. "It was probably for the best. A prison is no place for babies. They need sunlight and green grass and . . . But they brought him to see me every month and he seemed to be well taken care of. Davy was plump and healthy and—" Her voice broke. "Beautiful. Dear God, he is so beautiful."

"My son, Mary?" Jake asked hoarsely.

"Who else?" Mary blinked back the tears as she turned to face him. "Pallal was overjoyed when he found out I was pregnant. Another weapon to use against you. He knew you probably wouldn't give a damn about a child from a one-night stand, but he made sure I kept Davy long enough so that I'd do anything to get him back."

Jake's face had turned pale. "I would have cared. I do care. You know that."

She shook her head. "I don't know that. We were strangers. We're still strangers. You were probably grateful I passed so easily out of your life. Pallal was right: It was just a one-night stand we both knew wouldn't—"

"Don't tell me what I know," Jake said harshly. "It may have been just a one-nighter to you, but—" He broke off and then started again, "But it wasn't, dammit. It did mean something to you. I know it."

"It meant something to the Mary Harland I was three years ago," she said quietly. "But she doesn't exist any longer."

Jake's stare narrowed on her face. "I think she does exist. And I'm damn well going to find her." His gaze fell on the black jewelry box in her hand. "I suppose you were going to send a message to Pallal and make an offer of exchange."

She nodded. "The first phone call was to the warehouse. I didn't even know if the building was still there; they might have pulled it down or something. I was to contact Pallal as soon as possible to give him the information about your point of departure." She moistened her lips with her tongue. "He'll have to give me Davy, won't he? I just have to be firm. If he wants the Princess so badly, he'll give me my son."

"What was the name of the woman Pallal gave the boy to?"

"I don't know. He wouldn't tell me." Mary's gaze flew to his face. "Why?"

"I'm not taking the chance of Pallal not wanting the necklace enough." Jake turned away. "I'm going after my son."

Mary felt a wild leap of hope. "How?"

"I'll send a few men to ask discreet questions among the villagers this afternoon. It can't be common for Pallal to foster a child out to someone in the village."

"And then?"

"When I find out where he is, I'll take him and bring him to you."

It sounded so simple, Mary thought. So blessedly, miraculously simple. Davy. "What if Pallal has him guarded?"

Jake's lips tightened grimly. "I hope he does. I'm in a mood to crunch a few heads." He moved toward the door leading to the street. "One last question. You were seriously dehydrated when we found you. That was no setup."

"Pallal wanted it to look legitimate," she said simply. "There's a place at the prison called the hot box. He kept me there without water for two days."

Jake stared at her silently for a moment, his face shuttered. "I see." He opened the door. "We'll be leaving tonight. Try to get some rest."

"Jake."

He glanced over his shoulder.

Her eyes were shining brilliantly in her pale face. "Thank you."

"For God's sake, he's my kid too." Jake gave her a level look. "And you're wrong. We were never strangers and I'm not going to let you make us into strangers now, Mary."

She gazed after him and felt the faint stirring of

warmth again, stronger this time, as if something long frozen were beginning to melt.

She sat down in the chair and nervously linked her hands together. He had told her to rest, but how could she?

He was going to bring Davy to her.

"Jake phoned and said to tell you that you were to come with me." Bruno stood in the doorway, his face expressionless. "Hurry, please. We don't have much time."

Mary jumped up from the chair, her gaze fixed eagerly on Bruno. "Is everything all right? He's been gone so long. Is Davy—"

"Jake didn't say anything more. He was in a hurry." Bruno opened the door. "Only that we're to meet him at the yacht in an hour."

"Then everything must have gone well." Mary moistened her lips nervously. "He knows I wouldn't leave without—" She broke off and drew a deep breath. "I have to call Pallal."

"No." Bruno's face immediately hardened with suspicion. "I think we'll just leave the Colonel without any fond farewells."

"Oh, for heaven's sake, if I wanted to betray Jake do you think I'd tell you I was planning on calling Pallal?"

Bruno's expression didn't change and Mary went on, "Pallal told me to phone and tell him whether Jake was going to be leaving by air or ship. Does he know where the yacht's moored?"

Bruno shook his head.

"How long will it take to get into international waters?"

"Three hours, maybe."

"And one hour to get to the yacht. Five hours should be safe." She glanced at the small clock on the nightstand by the bed. "It's eight-thirty now. I'll tell Pallal that Jake's leaving by air at three A.M. That should keep him from sending the coast guard to scour the area until we're safely away. Where's the phone?"

"There's one in the shop across the street."

"Then let's go." She moved toward the door.

As he hesitated, she said impatiently, "I'll let you stand beside me and listen to every word I say."

He nodded grimly. "You can bet I'll be there." He held the door open for her to precede him. "The yacht."

"What?"

"Tell him we're taking the yacht."

"But why should I tell him—" Her gaze flew to his face. "You *lied* to me. We're going by air."

He nodded. "There was a slight chance you might have been able to slip a message to Pallal and I wanted it to be the message I wanted sent."

"You didn't trust me." She shrugged wearily. "Well, why should you?"

"It's my business to distrust people." For an instant Bruno's expression softened. "No offense. I know you've had a tough time. I just couldn't risk having Jake's neck chopped because I wasn't careful."

"No offense taken." She found herself smiling at him. You could hardly resent a man for being too loyal. "Now, may I make that call?"

• • •

Forty minutes later they were driving into the out-skirts of south Tarbol. "A private airport?" Mary asked.

"Very private. One runway. Jake used it for—" Bruno stopped before finishing. "In his business."

"Smuggling?"

He shrugged. "The government's put a high tariff on everything from foodstuffs to luxury items because they wanted a cut of every pie. Jake just took their cut and still sold the goods to the consumers at a lower price. Everyone benefited but the crooks in the bureaucracy."

"No wonder Pallal hates him. Pallal's a greedy man."

"A bastard," Bruno agreed. "I'm surprised Jake's leaving without taking him out of the game. He doesn't usually leave loose ends dangling."

"You've known Jake a long time?"

"Long enough." He glanced at her. "You and I have something in common. He bribed me out of a jail in Hong Kong."

"Jail?"

He nodded. "I got into a fight in a bar and clobbered the wrong guy. He happened to be the brother of the police commissioner. Jake was in the fight, too, but on the other side."

"And he still put up a bribe to get you out?"

"Jake never holds a grudge as long as the fight's fair. He knew they'd keep me in there till hell froze over, so he bought me out and put me to work for the organization to pay off the debt. I've been working for him ever since."

Mary looked out into the darkness. Surely they should be seeing some sign of the airstrip by now. She nervously wiped her clammy palms on her tunic. Bruno hadn't actually known if Davy was with Jake at the airport. What if something had gone wrong?

"You can count on Jake," Bruno said quietly, as if he'd read her mind.

Mary glanced sidewise to see him looking at her with sympathy. "Can I?" she whispered. "Davy's so important to me."

"And you're important to Jake," Bruno said. "He nearly went bonkers three years ago when he heard about that plane crash. We even went out to the crash site in the desert— It was just a blackened, broken hulk of metal. I remember Jake's face. . . ." He made a sudden turn and the Jeep left the road to bump over hard-packed sand. "The strip's just ahead, beyond that grove of palm trees."

Mary sat up straight, every muscle taut with tension. Bruno was drawing up beside a dark sedan parked beside the landing strip, and across the tarmac she caught a glimpse of the sleek outline of a small jet. The field was unlighted, but she could dimly discern several huge fuel-storage tanks across the runway, and at the far end of the runway a shack that served as a terminal or storage building. Beside the doorway of the shack she could see the shadowy outline of a familiar figure.

She jumped out of the Jeep before it stopped rolling and hurried across the tarmac. The man standing near the doorway of the shack was Jake, but there was no sign of Davy. Panic tightened her throat, nearly choking her.

"My son . . ." She stopped before Jake. "Where's Davy?"

"On board the plane."

Relief streamed through her. "Thank God." She started to turn toward the jet and then stopped to look at him uncertainly. "You're telling me the truth? This isn't just a trick to get me on board the plane?"

He stiffened as if she'd struck him. "Do you think I'd use my son as a carrot on a stick?"

She couldn't see his expression in the dark, but she knew she'd hurt him. "I knew you wanted me out of the country."

"I wouldn't lie to you. Davy's on board the plane. So is his foster mother. Her name is Kalana Jablar."

"You brought the woman who—"

"She's nuts about the boy and she's only a kid, barely seventeen, no family." He made an impatient gesture with one hand. "Think about it, Mary. When Pallal found out she'd handed him over to me, he'd probably have had her shot—or worse."

"I'm not arguing with you. I was just surprised."

"Hey, Jake, going camping?" Bruno was beside them, his gaze on the canvas pack strapped to Jake's back.

"Never hurts to be prepared." Jake's gaze was focused on the road that winded through the palm grove. "Get her on board the plane, Bruno. I told them to start the engines as soon as you arrived."

But Mary was already hurrying across the tarmac toward the steps leading up to the Lear jet. She heard Jake's low voice and then Bruno's shout of laughter behind her, but only on a subliminal level. Davy was on the plane. In a minute she'd see Davy again.

Kalana Jablar sat in a seat in the back of the plane holding Mary's sleeping son. She looked even younger than the seventeen Jake had said she was.

She wore a loose gold cotton caftan that comple-
mented the dark auburn of her hair but failed entirely to hide the almost painful slenderness of her
small figure. She clutched Davy closer as she saw
Mary. "You can't take him now. He's sleeping."

"I see that he is." Mary moved down the aisle to
stand beside the girl and look down at Davy. His
dark brown hair was tousled, but he had the silky
rosiness of a contented, healthy baby. Tears welled
in her eyes. "He's beautiful, isn't he?"

"I've taken very good care of him." The girl looked
at Mary with pride. "He loves me."

"I'm sure he does." For some reason the girl's very
defiance touched her. Jake had said she had nothing and no one, and now this child she loved was
being taken away, too, yet she was meeting this
latest deprivation with spirit and dignity. "And I
realize there are all kinds of things I need to learn
about him again. Perhaps you could help me?"

A flicker of joy crossed the girl's face, but she
quickly masked it behind a careless shrug. "I don't
see why not. Babies are easy." She stood up. "Sit
down and I'll let you hold him. Babies love to be
held, you know, even when they're sleeping. It makes
them feel safe." Her face became shadowed. "It's
important to feel safe."

"Yes, it is." Mary sat down in the seat across the
aisle and Kalana put the sleeping child in her arms.
He smelled of baby powder and was heavier than he
looked. Dear heaven, what a precious weight, Mary
thought. "He's grown so much since I last saw him."

"Yes." Kalana crossed her arms awkwardly across
her chest, as if she missed the familiar burden. "He
eats well. Some babies don't eat well at all. My brother

. . ." She stopped, sat back down in her chair, and said with pretended carelessness, "If you get tired of holding him, just tell me and I'll take him again."

"I won't get tired."

"No." Kalana's slim, nervous hands clutched at the arms of the seat. "I didn't think you would."

Bruno ran up the steps. "Start the engines!" he called into the cockpit.

The engines started to whine and he walked down the aisle toward Mary, his curious gaze on the baby. "Nice-looking kid." He stopped beside them and one big finger gently touched the boy's cheek. "You did good, Mary. Think he'll like St. Moritz?"

She swallowed and nodded. "St. Moritz? We're going to Switzerland?"

"Jake has connections there, and he thinks it's best to locate somewhere he can pull strings." He smiled crookedly. "After all, you, the baby, and Kalana have no passports. In fact, as far as the record goes, you died three years ago. It's not going to be easy to straighten all of that out."

"Will they even let us through Immigration?"

"No, that's why we're not landing at an international airport." He gently touched the baby's lips with his thumb. "Jake wants you settled comfortably before he starts to work on the legalities. He's afraid Pallal may try some string pulling himself to get you returned to Said Ababa before your identity is established."

"You mean we're being *smuggled* into Switzerland?"

Bruno grinned and nodded. "The classiest contraband we've ever handled. Don't worry—nobody is better at this than Jake."

"They're coming!" someone shouted from the cockpit. "Two cars."

"Buckle up," Bruno said tersely. "We're getting out of here."

"What? But why are—"

A beam of light suddenly highlighted Bruno's face through the window of the plane, and Mary's swift glance followed the beam to its source. Headlights. Two cars tearing through the palm grove toward the tarmac at tremendous speed.

"Pallal," she whispered.

The jet engines revved up to full power even as she spoke.

"Right. We've got to take off."

"Without Jake?"

"His choice. He's setting up a diversion. We'll come back for him."

"No!" She thrust the baby at Kalana and ran down the aisle toward the door. "Pallal hates Jake."

"Where the hell do you think you're going?" Bruno called after her. "Mary, dammit, Jake knows what he's doing."

"No, he doesn't. Pallal—" she ran down the steps just as the cars broke through the clearing. "Take off. Get Davy out of here!"

She heard Bruno cursing behind her as she tore across the tarmac toward the shack beside the runway where she'd last seen Jake. She heard the solid thunk as the door of the plane closed behind her.

The jet was taxiing down the runway, picking up speed, as she burst through the front door of the shack.

The shack was empty!

"Jake!"

The back door opened and Jake stood silhouetted in the doorway.

"Get out of there!"

She ran toward him across the room and out the back door. Jake grabbed her arm and half pulled, half dragged her, stumbling, running, through the palm grove.

A metallic rat-a-tat-tat.

The scream of the jet engines as the plane lifted from the ground.

The angry shouts of the men in the two cars as they pursued the plane down the runway.

"They're shooting at it," she sobbed, looking back over her shoulder. "Davy."

"It'll be out of range in seconds." Jake said. "They're safe." He pushed her down into a hollow of the ground, then fumbled with his backpack and brought out a black box. "Cover your head."

"Why should I cover—"

Jake pushed a button on the remote control.

The shack exploded into a fireball of flame, scattering burning debris over the runway and the entire clearing.

Stupefied, Mary gazed at the destruction.

Then, before she could fully take in what was happening, the oil tanks began to blow, one by one.

A river of black oil flooded the concrete tarmac, and behind it a hungry tongue of flame licked, pursued, devoured.

The two cars on the tarmac screamed to a halt, surrounded by flame and destruction on all sides.

"My God," Mary whispered.

Another oil tank blew, the explosion tossing the

black Mercedes onto its side as if it were a matchbox car.

The river of flame reached the gas tank of the Mercedes, as the occupants struggled to open the doors.

The car exploded!

The other car had reached the safety of the grove and was skidding desperately toward the road to Tarbol, trying to outrun the flames, which were already turning the tops of the palms into flaming umbrellas.

"Come on. We're not safe here anymore." Jake jumped up and jerked her to her feet. "Let's get out of this grove before it's torched."

Another explosion rocked the earth as they tore through the grove, heading not toward the road, but the desert.

Mary could hear Jake's labored breathing beside her and her own sobbing gasps as they fled through the flaming grove. The smell of oil and gritty smoke and burning trees filled her lungs.

The sand was suddenly softer, more resilient beneath the soles of her shoes, and the smoke was less dense.

"Can't we stop?" she gasped.

"No. Keep running and don't look back." They burst free of the grove and pounded across the sand, slipping and sliding on the deep dunes surrounding the palm grove.

Another blast shattered the earth and reverberated in the night air.

"How many . . ." She had no breath to finish.

He pulled her up to the top of the dune they were climbing, then pushed her into a reclining position on the other side. "One more. But I think we're far enough away to rest now. Though Lord knows, we can't—"

The final blast drowned the rest of his sentence and Mary could feel the rumbling echo quake and shift the loose sand beneath her body.

Her eyes widened as she looked down over the crest of the dune at the scene below. The grove was a solid sheet of flame mounting sixty or seventy feet in the sky. Thick black clouds of smoke rose in great sooty puffs.

"I can't believe it," she whispered. "What happened?"

"Plastic explosive. I set a little trap for Pallal."

"You expected him to follow us?"

"I thought there was a good chance he'd have a tail on you after you left him at the cafe. Pallal usually hedges his bets."

"And you never intended to go with us on the plane," she said wonderingly. "You meant the plane to leave you here."

Jake's features were stone hard in the stark, raging light of the flames. "I wanted Pallal."

She shivered as she remembered the exploding Mercedes. "And did you get him?"

"I don't think so. I think I caught a glimpse of him in the other car." He smiled coldly. "Next time."

Mary looked back at the grove. "Will he be back?"

"I doubt it. Why should he be? He thinks we all escaped in the jet." His gaze shifted to her face. "Why didn't you stay on the plane where I put you, dammit? You scared the hell out of me when I saw you running across the tarmac toward the shack."

"Pallal hates you. I knew what he'd do to you if he caught you."

"And do you think he'd be pleasantly disposed toward you?"

Her hands clenched into fists in the sand. "You helped me save Davy from him. I couldn't leave you here alone."

His gaze searched her face. "And that's all? Gratitude?"

"What do you expect me to say? I *am* grateful. Davy's safe now because of you." Her gaze anxiously searched the heavens. "He is safe, isn't he? Pallal can't do anything to stop the plane?"

Jake shook his head. "I told Bruno to head for Marasef in Sedikhan. It's right across the border, and the reigning sheikh isn't on cordial terms with Said Ababa."

Mary breathed a sigh of relief. "That's good."

A faint smile tugged at Jake's mouth. "You seem remarkably unworried about your own situation."

She realized suddenly that she wasn't at all anxious. She should have been terrified to be stranded in Said Ababa with Pallal still alive and seeking vengeance, but that was not the case. As long as Davy was safe and out of Pallal's hands, Jake and she could find a way to cope. "What do we do? Start walking for the border?"

The glance Jake gave her reflected amusement, admiration, and respect. "Now do I look like the sort of gent who would make a lady walk?"

She smiled, feeling suddenly lighthearted. "You stashed a camouflaged dune buggy over the next rise?"

He shook his head. "Too eye-catching. A Jeep." He stood up and dusted the sand from his jeans. "And now I believe we'd better make tracks. We have to be a hundred miles from here in four hours."

She stood up. "Where are we going? The border?"

"No." He took her elbow and began to propel her across the dunes. "The other way. Deeper into Said Ababa."

"Why?"

"There's an alternate landing field near the refineries at Danglor that we used for my business ventures."

Mary's gaze flew to his face. "Bruno's not going to have the jet fly back into Said Ababa to pick us up? Davy will—"

"Easy," Jake interrupted. "Davy and the jet stay in Marasef. I arranged for a helicopter to be gassed up and ready at Marasef airport the minute the jet touched down. Bruno will take the helicopter and pick us up at Danglor in four hours."

"I see."

"And we'll be back on our flight plan to St. Moritz in four hours after that."

They had reached the Jeep, and as Jake lifted Mary into the passenger seat he gravely met her gaze. "Only gratitude, Mary?"

She avoided his glance. "Of course, what else?"

His lips brushed the tip of her nose before he reached over to fasten her seat belt. "You might make a mental list of possibilities while we're on our way to Danglor." He ran around the Jeep and slid beneath the wheel. "Who knows? You might stumble across a reason that may surprise you."

He didn't wait for a reply as he turned on the ignition, put the Jeep in gear and carefully began negotiating the terrain.

• • •

The silver and cream-colored helicopter hovered and then slowly descended onto the tarmac. This field, like the other outside Tarbol, had no landing lights, but the first pale fingers of dawn were probing the night sky and the helicopter landed with no mishap.

Even before the cockpit door was thrown open, Jake was hurrying Mary across the tarmac toward the helicopter.

The wind from the rotors tore at her hair as she ducked beneath the blades. Bruno leaned out and lifted her easily into the copter even as he looked over her head at Jake and ruefully shook his head. "I couldn't help it, Jake. She was out of the plane before I could blink. I wasn't expecting her to pull a crazy stunt like that."

"Neither was I." Jake jumped into the copter and settled into the seat beside Mary. "We've already had a discussion regarding the nuances of her decision to come to my rescue."

Bruno sat back down in the pilot's seat. "Did you get Pallal?"

"No."

"Tough luck." The helicopter began to lift from the ground. "We saw the bonfire from the air. It was one hell of a farewell salute to Said Ababa."

Farewell. Mary's heart lifted with hope as she realized that they were actually on their way out of this hideous country. The government that had killed her father, the prison of Balahar would all be behind her. In a few hours she and Davy would be free. Tears filled her eyes.

"Hey." Jake's gaze was fixed intently on her face. "You okay, mate?"

"Fine." she drew a quivering breath. "I just realized it's almost over. I feel a little shaky."

"I'd say you have reason." He reached over, unfastened her seat belt and pulled her close to him, cradling her head on his shoulder. "Why don't you take a little snooze?" His hand gently stroked the hair back from her temple. "And when you wake up we'll be landing in Marasef. Okay?"

She should not be taking comfort from Jake, she thought. He would not understand that this moment of momentary weakness meant nothing.

He passed his hand over her eyes, closing them with firm gentleness. "St. Moritz." His voice came softly in the darkness behind her closed lids. "Think of St. Moritz. White snow and jagged mountains that plunge straight down into blue mountain lakes, chalets perched on the sides of—"

"Avalanches."

"Shut up, Bruno."

"Just thought I'd help out."

"Skiing, hang gliding."

"I'll shut up."

"Clean cold air. Stillness. Think St. Moritz."

Mary found herself relaxing against him, letting go of the memories, letting go of Said Ababa.

The thirty-room redwood and glass chalet appeared carved out of the side of the mountain, with a redwood deck that jutted out over an abyss and offered a stunning view of the valley below.

"It looks like something designed by Frank Lloyd

Wright," Mary said as she entered the gigantic foyer. "Very impressive."

Jake shrugged. "It's comfortable." He turned to Kalana. "Bruno will show you to a suite, and then I'd like you to go with him into town to choose everything needed for a nursery. You might pick up some clothes for you and Mary as well." He turned to Bruno, who was holding a delighted Davy over his head and making faces at him. "If Bruno can bear to stop that horseplay with my son, that is."

Bruno didn't look at him as he swung the gurgling baby over his head again. "I'll think about it. What a neat toy, Jake. We should have gotten one of these years ago."

"Leave the baby here when you go to town," Jake said dryly. "I don't want him dropped into a snowbank."

"Who'll take care of—" Kalana stopped as she glanced at Mary. She nodded quickly and followed Bruno up the angling flight of stairs.

"I want to talk to you." Jake turned and led Mary into a long, high-ceilinged room furnished with a contemporary sense of elegance in scarlet, cream, and beige. "Sit down."

Mary shook her head. "I need to stand after that plane trip." She moved over to the huge stone fireplace across the room. She could feel Jake's gaze on her and tension gripped her muscles. "This is so different from Said Ababa. I haven't seen snow since I went skiing in Squaw Valley five years ago." She ran her fingers over the wood of the mantel. "I was never very good at it. Maybe I can—"

"I don't want to talk about skiing." Jake wearily rubbed the back of his neck. "Why are you so afraid of me? You weren't like this at the flat. I'm not about to pounce on you."

She met his gaze. "I'm just feeling uneasy. Everything's happened so fast. Even this house makes me uneasy after being in that cell all those years. There's too much *room*."

His lips quirked. "We could always put a bed in the closet for you." His smile faded. "We both have adjustments to make. I've never even thought about being a father."

"We won't bother you," she said quickly. "As soon as you can arrange for our papers, I'll take Davy and leave. It's what I intended all along."

"Oh, will you?" His lips twisted in a sardonic smile. "Just 'How d'ya do? You have a son, my lad,' and then good-bye?"

"Davy's *my* son. He's the only thing that made me want to keep on living in that place. I won't give him up."

"Or share him? You seem willing enough to share him with Kalana. Why not with me?"

She stared at him.

"What are you thinking about? Talk to me."

"I'm confused. I never thought beyond escaping from Balahar and taking Davy out of Said Ababa. Every thought, all my energy was just aimed at one goal. I'd have done anything to get Davy."

He smiled grimly. "I know."

"Perhaps if I went away by myself and thought about everything, it would become clearer. I suppose you do have some rights where Davy's concerned."

"Do I?" He shook his head. "You're not leaving me again. I let you go once before and look what happened. This time we're going to settle our problems together." He went over to the large floor-to-ceiling window and looked unseeingly out at the breathtaking panorama. "I want you to marry me."

"Because of Davy? That would only complicate matters."

"I want him to have my name." He grimaced. "Such as it is. I don't have any idea who my parents were. I chose the last name myself when I was old enough to need one to get in the army. But later I went through the legal formalities and it's mine now. I want to give it to you both, if you'll have it."

Mary felt a wave of poignant tenderness, as unexpected as it was intense. "It's a fine name, Jake," she said gently. "Thank you for offering it, but—"

"You don't want it." He finished for her. "All right, let's get down to business. You *need* my name, Mary. When Pallal staged that plane crash, you were declared officially dead, and all your father's property that wasn't snatched up by Pallal was distributed among various charity organizations."

"I have the Burgundy Princess."

"But to sell it, you have to prove identity and ownership, and it may be a year or two before we can do that. In the meantime, since you have no legal American status, Davy is a Said Ababan citizen." He met her gaze. "Which means Pallal can request he be extradited back to Said Ababa as a ward of the state."

"No!"

"I talked to my lawyer by phone on the plane," Jake said. "It's a possibility, Mary."

Terror clutched at her. "I'll run away. I'll disappear. He *won't* have him."

"Easy. If you marry me, I can pull some strings to

push through legal adoption papers that will make him my son, with my Swiss nationality."

"Is that legal?"

"We could tie the case up in court for the next ten years, whether it's legal or not. And that would give you time to prove your own identity and claim Davy."

"But if I don't have documentation how can I even be married?"

"I own a tiny island in the Mediterranean, off the coast of Greece. I built a hotel-casino there two years ago." He shrugged. "One of the nice things about owning an island is you can also make the laws that govern it. We could fly there tomorrow and be married the same day. Then we could fly back here the following day with documentation in hand."

It sounded reasonable. "I don't know." Her gaze clung to Jake's. "You wouldn't try to take him away from me?"

"For the Lord's sake, what kind of—" He halted and then said carefully, "No, I won't try to take him away from you. Once you've proved your claim, I won't contest the divorce or demand custody of Davy. I'll even put it in writing, if you like."

Oh dear, she had hurt him again. He couldn't understand what it was like to have no one in the world but a child. Or perhaps he could, she thought suddenly. He'd grown up on the streets hungry and more alone than she'd ever been in that prison. At least she'd had Davy. "I'm sorry. That won't be necessary," she said quietly. "I trust you, Jake."

"No, you don't." He smiled lopsidedly. "Trust me not at all, or all in all."

"What?"

"Tennyson."

Still another thing she had forgotten about him, the boy who couldn't read but had overcome his handicap with imagination and determination.

"But you will trust me, Mary." He turned and moved toward the door. "Come on, I'll show you to your suite. It adjoins mine." He shook his head as he saw her stiffen. "See? You don't really trust me."

"Things are different now."

"You mean you don't have to go to bed with me to save Davy from Pallal."

"I'm free, Jake. I don't think you know what that means to me. I'm not about to go into another prison, not even an emotional one."

"I'm not going to demand anything of you that you don't want to give, Mary. I'll just feel better having you close and the marriage will look less like a setup. Okay?"

"Okay." She smiled tentatively. "You've been very kind, Jake. I'm grateful."

"Grateful!" he repeated with sudden violence. "I don't want your gratitude. I want you back the way you were. I want you well and happy and—"

"We can't go back, Jake." She met his gaze. "I don't want a relation with you or any man. Particularly not with you. I want Davy, and peace, and most of all I want my freedom."

"I'd give you your freedom."

She smiled sadly. "Give? If freedom has to be given, it's not freedom. I do remember that night, Jake. I remember you swept me away like a tornado. You were the same way in the casino. You're a very dominant man. Maybe that girl of three years ago wouldn't have minded standing in your shadow, but I couldn't bear it. I have to have room to breathe."

"I don't remember smothering you."

"You didn't have the chance. And I can't give you the chance now. I've lost too much time already."

"So I'm condemned without a trial?"

"It wouldn't work, Jake."

"Want to bet, luv?" He didn't wait for an answer, but preceded her from the room across the foyer and up the stairs. "I wouldn't if I were you. House odds. They run against you, you know."

The wind blew with lazy gentleness against her face and brought with it the scent of flowers. The fragrance was intoxicating, Mary thought, but no more enchanting than the view from the hotel balcony. In the distance gentle hills rolled against a sky whose brilliance stunned the eye, while on the hotel grounds rows of purple lilac bushes lined the flagstoned walks of the garden and clustered around the dozens of reflecting pools scattered among the groves of trees.

"Do you like it?" Jake stood in the doorway leading to the bedroom. "Not as dramatic as the view from the chalet, but I thought the high rollers would appreciate something a little more restful when they left the tables."

"It is restful." Mary turned back to him with a smile. "No sharpness, no bustle. I could stay here for weeks."

He shook his head. "You complained of leaving Davy for even one day."

Her smile faded. "I want him to get to know me again. Kalana's wonderful with him, but I want to take care of him and feed him and—"

"There's time for all that," Jake said gently. "You have all the time in the world now."

"I do, don't I? That seems so strange." She straightened her shoulders as she turned back to him. "When does this ceremony take place?"

"This evening. I've invited Reverend Duclair to the hotel for dinner and we'll have the ceremony on the terrace afterward." He smiled. "By the way, I had the owner of the boutique in the lobby downstairs select a dress and accessories for you."

"You've taken care of everything. Thank you."

He frowned. "I have a habit of taking charge, but if you'd rather choose something yourself, send the things back. I just thought I'd make arrangements easier for you."

"No, I don't care. Anything's fine." She turned back to look at the verdant hills. "I seem to have trouble making decisions. For three years I had no control at all over my life, and suddenly I have choices."

"It will come easier. Just make one decision at a time." He moved to stand behind her. "When you wake up in the morning you decide whether you'll wear black shoes or brown shoes. Then you decide whether you'd like coffee or tea with your breakfast." His hands slid beneath her long hair and lifted its silky weight to bare her nape. "Whether to wear your hair up or down." The soft breeze touched her skin and sent a little shiver through her. He released her hair and, as it flowed down her back, he carefully tidied it, arranging the strands to his exact satisfaction. His touch was gentle, almost casual, but the act itself was somehow exquisitely intimate. He was so close she could feel the heat of his body and catch the spicy aroma of his after-shave. "Whether to come alive or stay locked in that mental prison Pallal built for you."

She drew a shaky breath as she stepped to the side and turned to face him. "You're right. One decision at a time. First, I'll go to the beauty salon downstairs and have something done with this shaggy mane a Saint Bernard wouldn't claim." She moved toward the door. "And then I'll call Kalana and make sure Davy's all right. That's two decisions in one minute. I'm making progress." She glanced back over her shoulder. "Shall I meet you in the lobby at seven?"

He nodded, his gaze intent on her face. "You're running away."

Color flooded her cheeks. "No, I'm not. I just have things to do before this evening."

"I don't mind you running away." A slow smile lit his face. "It's a good sign. You have to feel threatened to want to run away."

She stiffened. "I don't see you as a threat."

"You didn't at the beginning. You saw me first as an escape and then as someone who'd return your son to you. But now that you've had a chance to get your breath, you're seeing me a little differently, aren't you?"

"Sex? I've never denied you arouse me."

"Denial would be a waste of time. But not only sex, Mary. Choice. You're so high on your freedom. Well, choice is the first ingredient of freedom. You're seeing me as the first man you chose to make love to. You'll recall that I never coerced you. You're seeing me as the man you wanted so badly three years ago that you didn't want to wait to get out of the elevator."

She gazed at him, stunned. The shock of his words

tore through her, bringing with it the memory of those first moments of passion: his fingers opening her blouse, looking at her, his mouth moving on her flesh. She felt a pulsating heat between her thighs and the muscles of her stomach clenched tightly. Her physical response surprised her as much as the stark boldness of his sentence, and she hurriedly turned away. "That was a long time ago. I'll . . . see you at seven."

She could feel his gaze on the center of her back as she moved across the suite toward the door leading to the corridor. She wasn't really running away, she assured herself. She knew what she wanted, and it wasn't Jake Darcy. She wanted Davy and freedom and perhaps later a career. She certainly didn't want the emotional turmoil and heady sensual enslavement Jake represented. A magnetic attraction of that strength could be a prison too. What she and Jake had experienced had been an explosive, dreamlike episode between two people who had nothing in common but thier sexuality.

No, she wasn't running away. She was merely being a survivor.

Six

After the ceremony Reverend Duclair gave them the required documents and departed with a smile and good wishes.

"He's a very nice man," Mary said as she watched the minister move toward the terrace door. "More the cozy parish priest type than Las Vegas justice of the peace. He told me you brought him and his wife from Jamaica and built a church for them here on the island."

"The islanders needed a minister. It was a benefit to the hotel guests too." His eyes were suddenly twinkling. "After I take their money at the casino, I offer them spiritual solace. It works out very well."

"No, really. Why did you bring him here?"

He didn't answer immediately. "I like a sense of substance connected with everything I own," he finally said quietly. "This hotel and casino may be gone tomorrow, but values endure."

"Are you a religious man?"

"I grew up in such a hodgepodge of Eastern and Western culture that it's difficult for me to believe completely in the philosophies of any one religion. But I have certain beliefs. Doesn't everybody? I believe there has to be something out there. I believe people should help each other." He looked up to meet her gaze. "And I believe in destiny. I've had proof of that truth."

Mary quickly lifted her glass of wine to her lips and nodded at the documents on the table. "Will you give the marriage license to your lawyer tomorrow?"

"As soon as we get back." Jake set his glass down and stood up. "Come for a walk in the garden with me." He smiled coaxingly. "Do you realize we've never taken a walk together?"

"That's hardly unusual. We've never done anything together except—" She stopped.

"Make love," he finished. To her relief, he didn't pursue or take advantage of her gaffe. "But you're wrong. We've done other things." He pulled her to her feet and led her across the terrace toward the stone steps leading down to the garden. "Let's see: We've danced together, we've eaten together, we've taken a shower together. We've ridden in a car together. When you consider, all of those activities qualify as a courting ritual." His gaze moved over her. "I like that lacy dress. You wore white the first time I saw you."

"I'd rather not talk about that night." She hurriedly changed the subject. "When we get back to St. Moritz I'd like to arrange for a tutor for Kalana. She says she hasn't been to school for over five years." Mary's brow furrowed. "But that's all I can get out of her. She won't talk about herself or her family. But she appears very bright, doesn't she?"

Jake nodded. "She was quick to grasp the situation and all its implications when I came to the cottage. She's evidently used to coping and making the best of life."

"What was the cottage like?"

"Tiny, shabby, immaculately clean. No family pictures or memorabilia. When we left she packed only the baby's things and a few clothes for herself and left the house without a backward glance."

"Strange."

"Not so strange. There are a hell of a lot of orphans in Said Ababa, thanks to their so-called benevolent dictatorship. Children learn to accept what they're given and make the best of it."

"Like you did?"

He shook his head. "I couldn't accept anything. I always had to have more, be more. It made life a hell of a lot harder for me."

"But you wouldn't have had it any other way."

"No, I guess not." He grinned. "But it's easier to say that in retrospect than to live through it. The school of hard knocks is good training, though. I learned not to give up until the last vote was in."

"I learned that too. For the first few months I couldn't believe I'd be able to live through another week in Balahar without going insane. Then I realized if I died or went crazy, Pallal would win. I couldn't let that happen." She stopped beside one of the shimmering mirror-like pools, gazing at their images in the water. How odd she looked, she thought; the pampered, polished woman reflected in the pool wasn't someone who should know anything about death and prisons. "So I began to do what I had to do to survive."

"The vacuum."

"It was easier after Davy came. He made living worthwhile. I think all babies must do that." She started to walk again. "They show us there's hope."

They walked on in silence for a long time, but Mary didn't find the quiet discomforting. Jake was a solid, safe presence in the darkness. It was queer that one moment she could find him so disturbing as to make her uneasy and the next there was only a companionable bond. Yet it had also been like that before, she remembered suddenly. In between explosive bursts of passion, he'd been caring, friendly, even cosseting.

"I don't suppose you'd consider sleeping with me tonight?" Jake asked quietly.

Her gaze flew to his face.

"Just sleeping," Jake said. "I'd like to hold you."

"That wouldn't be a very good idea."

"You can trust me."

She looked at him skeptically.

"All right." He chuckled. "I agree. We're both too combustible to make guarantees. I just kind of liked the idea. I won't push." He added, "Yet."

"I think I'll go back to the hotel." She turned and started quickly down the flagstoned path. "It's late and I'm tired."

"It's not even ten o'clock and you're telling a whopper, luv." He caught up with her in two long strides. "But that's okay. I knew I'd run the risk of putting you on the defensive again. I should have waited." His face was suddenly taut in the moonlight. "I thought I was a patient man, but I guess I'm not where you're concerned."

She didn't answer and they silently went back to the hotel.

* * *

"No, you rascal, you can *not* eat the snow." Mary carefully wiped the snow from Davy's face with a tissue. He promptly buried his face back in the snow pile in front of him. "Davy!" She began to laugh helplessly. In his red-hooded snowsuit he looked like Santa Claus's helper and now the snow beard completed the picture. "We'd better take him in, Kalana. He's impossible. I think he's trying to dig a cave and hibernate."

Kalana was chuckling, too, as she snatched the squealing child up from the snow and gave him a hug. "As soon as there's a fresh snowfall we'll make him some snow ice cream. Maybe that will satisfy him."

"I doubt it." Mary stood up and dusted the snow from her orange ski suit. "He's obviously in love with the stuff. Look at him. He's so happy he's glowing."

Kalana nodded. "He likes it here." She hoisted the toddler onto her shoulders and fell into step with Mary as they started back toward the chalet. "So do you." She glanced at Mary with a smile. "You're not the same as when you came here six weeks ago. You're like Davy."

"What do you mean?"

"You're beginning to glow."

Mary chuckled. "It's all this frigid air. I feel like Rudolph the Red-Nosed Reindeer."

"No, I think it's because you're happy. You look . . ." Kalana hesitated. "Well, there aren't any shadows anymore."

Mary's smile faded as she thought about Kalana's words. Had she changed in these last weeks? She certainly felt strong physically. The weeks of skiing, skating, and taking walks with Davy and Kalana had given her a stamina and a youthful exuberance she'd thought she'd lost forever. "What about you, Kalana? Are your shadows gone?"

Kalana quickly looked away. "I feel very well."

"But are you happy?" In these weeks Mary had grown very fond of the girl. Kalana was energetic and intelligent and on occasion displayed a mischievous sense of humor that surprised Mary. Yet she never totally lost that fragile air of being one of the lost ones of the world.

Kalana was silent a moment. "You want everyone to be happy. I'm content. Isn't that enough?"

"No. Girls your age should be happy. Work on it."

Kalana laughed and nodded. "I'll try. You and Jake have certainly provided me with everything to make me happy. I have lessons, food, a comfortable place to live." She swung the baby down from her shoulder to the ground and slowed her pace to accommodate the toddler. "And Davy. You still let me have Davy."

"What would we do if you weren't here?" Mary asked lightly. "Davy would be lost without you."

"Would he?" For an instant a poignant wistfulness crossed Kalana's face. "Babies forget so quickly. Already he loves you more than he does me." She went on hurriedly, "As is right and proper. You gave him birth."

"And you gave him care and love."

"Yes." With an effort, Kalana smiled. "Still, it would be very nice to come first with someone." Kalana started trotting, pulling the chortling baby after her. "Come on, let's get him inside and changed. It's almost time for his nap."

Jake was waiting on the redwood deck when they reached the steps.

He was back! Mary experienced an instant of shock, followed immediately by a wild mixture of feelings. He'd been in Washington for more than two weeks and she hadn't realized until this moment how much she'd missed seeing him, hearing his voice, watching him move lazily across a room. Not that she had seen very much of him since they had come back to St. Moritz. He appeared to be deliberately absenting himself from the chalet. If he was not touring his properties and casinos, he was closeted with lawyers. But this was the longest time he'd been away.

He was coatless, wearing only blue jeans and a navy and white ski sweater, and Mary felt a twinge of impatient concern. For goodness sake, it was thirty degrees and they were all bundled up like Eskimos and Jake still refused to wear a jacket. "You'll get pneumonia," she said as she picked Davy up and climbed the steps toward him. "This isn't your balmy Greek island."

"Pneumonia is a virus. You don't get it from becoming chilled." Jake took Davy and gave him to Kalana. "I need to talk to Mary, Kalana. Will you take care of Davy?"

Jake had barely glanced at the baby, Mary thought. She had noticed before that he never held or played with the baby, as Bruno was fond of doing. Well, she supposed some men just took to small children and some didn't.

Kalana nodded and disappeared into the house with Davy.

"Something's wrong?" Mary's gaze searched his face. "You've heard something from Said Ababa?"

"Nothing's wrong that can't be fixed." He took her arm and led her toward the door. "Come into the kitchen. When I saw you playing in the snow I made hot chocolate. You look like you could use a cup."

She nodded absently as she wiped the soles of her snowy boots on the outside rug and followed him into the house. "It's icy cold. Don't you feel it?"

"I like the cold." Jake led her down the corridor toward the kitchen. He glanced at her rosy cheeks and sparkling eyes. "I've lived in hot countries all my life. You seem to enjoy it, too."

"I do." As they entered the kitchen she took off her ski jacket and dropped it onto the back of one of the kitchen chairs. "I like everything about this place. The space, the quiet, the crunch of the snow as I walk." she crossed the room and took down two mugs from the cabinet above the stove. "And especially the taste of hot chocolate when coming in from the cold." She poured two cups from the pot and tossed in marshmallows. "Thanks. It was thoughtful of you to make hot chocolate, Jake."

"I'm a thoughtful guy." Jake sat on a kitchen chair and stared down at the frothy chocolate. "You're looking very well."

"I feel well. Did you have a good trip?"

"Yes and no."

Mary tensed. "What's the problem?"

"Pallal has laid a claim on behalf of the Said Ababan government to extradite Davy."

"We expected that to happen." She moistened her lips. "But the Swiss government will pay no attention to the claim, right?"

"Right. I just wanted you to know." He smiled. "And the good news is that I think we can expect your identity papers to be issued within three months."

"Wonderful." She relaxed. "You were so serious I was afraid something had gone wrong."

"No, I was worried about something else." He looked down at his hot chocolate. "Bruno says you won't go to town. Not even to take Davy to the doctor."

"Kalana takes him for his checkups." Mary's gaze slid away from Jake's. "I prefer to stay here."

"I don't like it."

"Too bad." She stood up. "I think I'll go see how Davy—"

"Sit down, Mary."

She started for the door. "I'll see you at dinner."

"We're going out to dinner."

She stopped and looked back at him. "Where?"

"The casino in St. Moritz."

"No, it will be too—"

"Crowded? Yes, it will be crowded. It's Friday night and the casino's very popular."

"I'll stay here, thank you."

"Oh no, luv." He stood up and moved forward to stand before her. "You'll go with me. I've invited an important official from the American Embassy to meet us there. He could be very useful in safeguarding Davy's position here."

"Invite him to the chalet."

"The casino or nothing."

"Why are you doing this? I don't want to go to the casino."

"That's why I have to force you to go. Do you think I like acting the bad guy? I have enough going against me without this."

"Then leave me alone."

"I can't." He gently pushed back a strand of hair from her cheek. "Look, after Bruno told me you wouldn't leave here I started putting two and two together. I remembered how scared you were after you came back from getting the Princess. I thought at the time it was me you were frightened of, but that wasn't it. You're scared of crowds."

"I'm just not used to them. Balahar—"

His lips tightened. "I know why you're like this. Chalk another one up for Pallal. But it doesn't matter why. You can't give in to it or it will become an entrenched phobia. I won't let Pallal do that to you. He's already damaged you enough."

"I'll be fine. I just need time to adjust."

"You've had six weeks."

"I did very well when we went to the island to be married."

"It was the off-season. The hotel was only half full." He shook his head. "No crowds."

He was relentless. She felt the panic rising within her. "I know what's best for me. I'll go when I please."

"All right." His hand dropped away from her hair. "If you think Davy's safe enough without the power of the American Embassy behind him."

"*Damn* you, Jake."

"Once more, with feeling."

"This isn't funny."

"I didn't think it was. That's why I'm being such a horse's ass about it."

"You really won't bring the man here?"

"I really won't," he said gently. "Don't be afraid. I'll be there."

"It won't make any difference."

"It always makes a difference to have a hand to hold."

She glared at him. "And to think I was actually glad to see you."

"Were you? Then I'm making progress." He smiled at her. "After you get over being mad at me, we'll have to discuss it." He turned and moved to the door. "We should leave at eight. Wear that pretty lacy white dress, will you, luv? You looked sweet in it."

Before she could speak he was gone.

Mary drew a deep breath and found her hands were clenched into fists at her sides. She consciously relaxed them and followed him from the room. She couldn't remember ever being this angry. She accepted that a good part of the anger was generated by fear, but she also resented Jake's blackmail. She had promised herself she would never be coerced again, and Jake had taken away her choice and made her feel helpless. Jake would have to be taught that she wouldn't submit to being treated like a child who had to be told what was good or bad for her.

She turned and took the cups to the sink and poured out the remains of the chocolate, her brow furrowed in thought.

Mary bent over and kissed Davy's forehead. "He feels warm."

Kalana shook her head. "He's fine. He ate a good dinner and dropped off while he was in the tub. It's all that playing in the snow." She tilted her head and stared at Mary. "You don't look like yourself."

"Bad?"

"No, just different. When I picked out that gown I

didn't think it would look like it does on you. You don't . . ." She paused, thinking about it.

"What? Look wholesome?"

"Well, certainly not wholesome, but . . ."

"Good. Sweet?"

Kalana shook her head.

"Even better." Mary kissed Kalana's cheek. "You've made my night. I'll be back early. Keep a close eye on Davy, okay?"

"He's fine," Kalana repeated. "You're getting paranoid."

"Talk to Jake. He'll probably agree with you. He already thinks I'm a little unbalanced." Mary turned and picked up her crimson lamé cloak from the chair by the door. "Let's just show him he's wrong."

Kalana frowned. "Jake doesn't think you're—"

"Oh, but he does. Good night, Kalana."

Mary shut the door and walked down the hall toward the staircase. She could feel the tension coiling within her and the palms of her hands were icy cold.

Jake was waiting for her in the foyer, startlingly handsome in a tuxedo. His eyes widened as he watched her descending the staircase. "You—you didn't wear the white dress."

"I decided I'd rather wear this one. Do you have any objection?"

Jake's gaze traveled over the crimson lamé halter gown that lovingly followed every hill and valley of Mary's figure. "It doesn't look like something you'd choose."

"Kalana chose it. She can't wear red herself but she loves the color. At first I thought it was a mistake, but I've changed my mind." She handed him her cloak. "Everyone needs an occasional change of image."

"Well, you certainly succeeded in—Lord!"

She had turned around to reveal that the back of the gown was cut a good two inches below the waist.

He quickly put the cloak over her shoulders. "If you want to avoid crowds you've picked the wrong gown to do it," he said grimly. "Every lecher in the place will be nuzzling up to you."

"Really?" She fastened the button at the throat of the cloak. "Do you think they'll offer me a hand to hold?"

His gaze narrowed on her face. "Is that what this is all about? You're angry with me and you want to see me burn a little?"

"I only want to establish that I wear what I wish to wear." She met his gaze. "You can't have everything your way, Jake."

"And you wish to wear a dress that's designed to turn me on." Jake's lips tightened. "Don't you know I get hard just looking at you in that damn unisex ski suit? What do you think you're doing to me in that gown?"

She turned away. "You have your problems, I have mine." She moved toward the door. "Shall we go? I want to get this over with."

"So do I." Jake strode past her and flung open the door. "This was a mistake, Mary."

"That's what I tried to tell you," Mary said as she went past him onto the deck. "You wouldn't listen."

"Well, you've certainly caught my attention now."

People.

Mary stood in the luxurious foyer of the casino and tried to breathe deeply, evenly.

The large area was thronged with women in fashionable gowns and men in tuxedos.

Shrill voices.

Smoke.

The sound of slot machines.

Music from the adjoining cocktail bar.

"Mary?"

She turned to Jake and thrust her cloak blindly at him. "Where is he?"

"We're to meet him in the lounge." Jake's gaze searched her face. "All right?"

"No." She couldn't *breathe*. "But you wouldn't care about that."

"I do care," he said quietly, taking her elbow. "But it's got to be done. Let's go." He handed her cloak to an attendant and propelled her through the crowd toward the cocktail lounge. "Easy does it, luv."

Easy? There was no air. She was smothering. Her head was ringing from the sounds of laughter and chatter.

In the bar it was worse. The place was wall-to-wall people. Smoke, noise, music. Too much noise.

"This is Mr. Danolde, Mary." Jake had stopped beside a graying man in a dark blue business suit. She was vaguely aware he had a tan, from skiing no doubt, and nice brown eyes.

She heard herself murmur an acknowledgment of the introduction, and then they were sitting down on the velvet cushions of a booth across from the bar.

Jake and Danolde were talking.

She sat there with a smile pasted on her lips.

The music blared. The glassware clinked.

Laughter. The noise was deafening.

Danolde said something to her. Panic surged through her as she realized she couldn't hear him.

Suddenly the noise was gone and she could hear nothing!

Jake was answering, distracting Danolde's attention, and then Danolde was rising to his feet, saying something else. She could see his lips move but she couldn't understand the words.

She smiled and murmured something polite.

Danolde was gone.

Jake leaned toward her, speaking urgently.

She couldn't hear him!

She couldn't hear anything but the pounding of her heart and the blood racing through her veins.

She jumped up from the cushioned seat and ran through the lounge. People stared at her as she shoved through the crowd.

She couldn't hear the music any longer.

She couldn't hear the voices.

She could hear nothing and the silence terrified her more than the noise.

She was outside on the sidewalk. The doorman blew his whistle for a taxi.

She couldn't hear it.

She was running, the tears streaming down her cheeks.

Headlights shone on the icy street, blinding her. Gaudy neon reflected pink on the snowbanked sidewalk.

A hand grasped her shoulder. She fought it.

Jake. It was Jake.

Jake holding her, talking to her, his lips pressed to her temple.

". . . scared me to death."

She could *hear* him.

Relief surged through her. She sagged against him, holding him tightly.

"It's okay, Mary." Jake's voice was soothing. "You're fine. Everything's fine."

"The hell it is," Mary whispered. "Mr. Danolde?"

"You were great." Jake rubbed her wet cheek with his handkerchief. "You knocked his socks off. He likes red too."

She laughed shakily. "I thought I was going deaf. I couldn't hear anything."

"Hysteria."

"I'm *not* a hysteric."

"You just got scared," Jake said gently. "You blocked out everything you didn't want to hear. You nearly gave me a heart attack."

"It serves you right." Mary took the handkerchief from him and wiped her face. "You shouldn't meddle with people's phobias if you don't want to get caught in the aftershock."

"I had to meddle. I couldn't let you go on."

"Couldn't you have broken me in a little easier? Say a visit to the local Swiss version of McDonald's at three o'clock in the morning?"

"I didn't think you were this bad," he said simply. "When you went after the Burgundy Princess you were out in worse crowds than at the casino tonight."

He was right, she realized in surprise. The experience in Said Ababa had been bad, but nothing like the traumatic one she had just undergone. Evidently her psyche had been busily manufacturing nightmare ways to protect itself. "Dear heaven, I *was* getting paranoid."

Jake took off his coat and draped it around her bare shoulders. "The only thing you're in danger of getting right now is hypothermia. Come on, I'll take you home."

"No."

He paused in buttoning the coat to look at her. "No?"

"I want to go back to the casino." She laughed shakily as she saw his shocked expression. "Well, I don't actually want to go. I've got to go."

She started back down the street toward the casino.

Jake fell into step with her. "Don't do this, Mary." He made a face. "If not for yourself, think of me. I don't believe I'm up to it."

"You? I'm shaking in my shoes. I thought I was going crazy in that lounge." She stopped before the casino. The doorman's whistle was blessedly shrill in her ears. "But I won't let myself fall apart like that. I won't be beaten." She unbuttoned his coat and handed it back to him. "You'd better take this. I hear this is a classy place. I don't think they'll let you in without a coat or tie."

"They'd let me in. I make the rules."

"So I noticed." She smiled with an effort. "But not with me, buster."

A slow smile lit his face as he put on the jacket. "That's been coming to my attention of late." He held out his hand. "Will you hold my hand? I'm bloody terrified to have you go in there again."

She put her icy hand in his, and waves of reassurance immediately enveloped her.

"Ready?" he asked.

She nodded and moved toward the glass door the doorman held open for them.

Noise.

People.

Music.

Her throat tightened with terror; her heart started to pound.

Jake's hand tightened on hers. "Okay, I've had it. Let's blow this joint."

She found herself laughing and the tension easing. "Not on your life. We're going into the lounge."

"You really know how to make it tough on a guy. Five minutes?"

"Fifteen." She moved toward the lounge.

"If you insist. Though I'll be on pins and needles. Speaking of pins and needles, did I ever tell you about the time I was caught by a tribe of Zulus and they pegged me out on an anthill?"

"Zulus?" Her eyes widened. "When was that?"

"When I was nineteen." He pushed her down in the booth. "That was in my mercenary days. I got separated from my unit and was captured by these tall, naked blighters who didn't half like me prowling around their hunting grounds. That was where the anthill came in. It was their ritual way to rid themselves of . . ."

Jake's words flowed on and Mary found herself leaning forward so as not to miss a syllable. The story was wry, convoluted, and fascinating.

"And that was when they poured the honey all over me." Jake glanced at his watch. "Time's up." He plucked her out of the booth and pushed her toward the lounge. "Let's go."

"You can't stop there," she protested as he half pulled her through the foyer. "Okay. You were pegged down, surrounded by Zulus, with honey poured all over you. How did you get out?"

"I didn't." Jake took her cloak from the attendant and put it around her shoulders. "Don't be silly. No one could get out of a situation like that."

"Then how—You *lied*."

"I merely exercised my talents as a storyteller. There's a difference." He grinned as he whisked her through the front door. "I had to do something to while away the time, since you were forcing me to stay there."

She started to laugh helplessly. "You're impossible, Jake."

"Exceptional, not impossible."

The Mercedes drew up in front of the casino and the parking attendant jumped out and handed Jake the keys.

Jake opened the passenger door. "On Saturday I'll take you to the circus and, if you're very good, I'll tell you about the time the KGB caught me trying to smuggle plans of their secret radar installation out of Russia."

She got into the car. "Another tall tale?"

"Well, I was in Russia six months." He smiled teasingly. "Suppose I let you make up your own mind." He slammed the door, came around to the driver's side of the car and slipped behind the wheel.

The garage door opened automatically and Jake drove into the five-car garage. He turned off the ignition and lights and started to open the driver's door.

"Wait." Mary reached out and touched his arm.

He turned to look at her. "Something wrong?"

"No." She hesitated. "I just wanted to say thank you."

He shook his head. "I bungled it. I nearly sent you round the bend."

"You meant well." She smiled. "And you were right—the longer I waited, the harder it would have been." She grimaced. "Though I can't imagine it being much worse."

"Agreed." His hands gripped the steering wheel. "I nearly went into a tailspin when I saw what I'd done to you."

"But then you held my hand, made me laugh, and you told me that outrageous story." Her smile widened. "I'm grateful for all of those things. I just wanted to let you know." She opened the car door and got out. "I owe you, Jake."

He got out of the car and came toward her. "So pay me already. I'm not proud." He stopped before her. "Any little token will do. The Burgundy Princess, your firstborn son." He paused. "A night in your bed."

The air suddenly crackled with tension. The levity vanished from his expression as he reached out and unbuttoned her cloak. "That damn gown's been bothering me all night. You wanted it to bother me, didn't you?"

"I was annoyed with you." Her voice sounded breathless. "But it was petty of me to—"

"No." He pushed the cloak off her shoulders and it fell into a glittering crimson pool at her feet. "Not petty," he said huskily. "An excuse."

"No."

"Think about it. You're not the kind of a woman who would tease a man. You're too honest." He stepped closer. "Just think about it, luv."

She couldn't think. He was too close. Too male.

Her emotions hadn't been dulled, but rather stimulated by the adrenaline-charged evening.

"I'm not asking for a commitment. Just come to bed and let me try to please you." His arms slipped around her, his fingertips tracing the naked hollow of her spine, gently rubbing, his fingertips warm silk on her flesh.

She shivered, instinctively moving nearer.

His lips feathered the pulse point beneath her chin as his fingers traveled slowly down her spine. "You're a responsive woman. You need this." His hands slid down past her waist, beneath the lamé of the gown to cup her buttocks. "And heaven knows, I do." He squeezed gently, then released and squeezed again. "Come, let me love you. Remember how it felt when you sat on my lap and let me hold you and—"

She took a step back and his hands slipped away from her.

"No?" he asked quietly.

She laughed shakily. "Lord, you're tough, Jake. I almost . . ." She shook her head skeptically. "No commitment?"

He grinned. "Well, not unless I could talk you into one by hook or crook." He pushed her toward the door leading to the hall. "Never mind, I just thought I'd give it a shot, since you were feeling the pangs of gratitude."

"You're absolutely imposs—"

"Stop right there."

She stopped, glancing over her shoulder, startled. "Why?"

"Because I can't resist . . ." He knelt down and pressed his lips to the hollow of her spine where her waist flowed into her buttocks. "I do like this hollow. I've been looking at it all evening." His warm tongue touched her flesh.

She inhaled sharply, her spine arching.

He stood up, his palm gently rubbing the spot his lips had caressed. "Ah yes, we're coming along nicely. Do think about us, Mary. I believe you'll come to some amazing conclusions."

He opened the door and let her precede him into the hall. "My door will be open and you'll get a warm welcome if you decide that—"

"Mary!"

Mary looked up to see Kalana leaning over the banister.

"Come quick! It's Davy!"

Seven

"What's wrong with Davy?" Mary ran up the stairs, scarcely aware that Jake was only a step behind her. "He's sick. I knew he was sick. I should have stayed home."

"It's my fault," Kalana said. "I should have taken his temperature, but he seemed so well and—"

"Have you called the doctor?" Jake asked.

Kalana nodded. "About an hour after you left, Davy woke up crying and he was burning up. The doctor's with him now."

"Why didn't you call me at the casino?" Mary said over her shoulder as she ran down the hall.

"I didn't think of it. I was so worried . . . I forgot he wasn't mine." Kalana ran after her. "I just held him and rocked him until the doctor came."

"You should have called me," Mary said fiercely. "He's mine. I had a right to be with him. He's *mine*."

Kalana looked as if she'd struck her. She paled. "I know."

"I'm sorry, Kalana." Mary shook her head. "I didn't mean . . ."

"She's frightened, Kalana," Jake said gently. "You should have called us."

Kalana nodded. "I know I should have remembered. I was frightened too. The doctor's not sure, but he thinks it might be pneumonia."

"Dear Lord," Mary said as she opened the door and hurried into the nursery.

It wasn't pneumonia, it was flu. Still dangerous for a child as young as Davy, but not serious enough for hospitalization. By the next night his fever had dropped to a little above normal and within forty-eight hours all that remained was an extremely cranky little boy.

"Go to bed," Jake said firmly when he came into the nursery at three-thirty in the morning and found Mary still in the rocker holding Davy. "He's almost well and you'll make yourself ill if you don't get some rest. You haven't slept more than a few hours in the past three days."

"Neither has Kalana." Mary leaned back in the rocker. "Davy just dropped off again, but he's only been taking catnaps. He keeps fretting and I don't want to wake her."

He stood looking at the two of them for a few moments before he suddenly moved forward. "Give him to me."

She looked at him in surprise. "But you—"

"He's my kid, isn't he?" He took Davy from her, balancing him in the curve of his arm while he pulled Mary to her feet. "It's time I took my turn."

She gazed at him doubtfully as he sat down in the rocker. He had just come back from the casino and was still dressed in the faultless elegance of his black tuxedo. Nothing could have looked more incongruous than him holding Davy. "Are you sure you know what to do?"

"I'm a bloody expert." He started rocking back and forth. "I delivered a baby once in Kenya."

A smile tugged at her lips. "To one of the Zulus who pegged you out for the ants?"

"No, to a poor little sod of a girl who was knocked up by one of the soldiers in my unit. She was crazy about him and followed him from her village and wouldn't go back."

"What happened?"

"He left her and the kid and went to Nicaragua." Jake pulled the blanket tighter around Davy. "Bastard didn't care if they starved."

Her gaze narrowed on his face. "But you did, I think."

He shrugged. "I couldn't do much. I was pretty broke in those days, but I managed to give her enough to get her back to her village and later to send her and the kid to the mission school." He frowned. "Why are you standing there? Go to bed."

She hesitated, still gazing at him uncertainly. Then she turned and left the room. In spite of her weariness she found she couldn't sleep more than a few hours. She woke after her nap and lay in bed for another twenty minutes before giving up the struggle to get herself back to sleep. Then she threw back the covers and headed for the shower.

Forty-five minutes later she quietly opened the door of the nursery.

Jake was still in the rocking chair; at some point he had shed his tuxedo jacket and rolled up the sleeves of his white dress shirt. Davy was sound asleep and Jake was looking down at him.

Mary inhaled sharply as she saw his expression.

Tenderness. Passionate, possessive tenderness illuminated his face as he looked down at Davy.

She must have made a sound, for he looked up and saw her.

"I didn't think you liked little children."

"I was scared," he said simply. "You kept talking about taking him away from me. I've never had anyone of my own and . . ." He met her gaze across the room. "I'd already found out how much it hurt to lose you. I didn't know if I could stand it happening again."

She could feel the tears stinging her eyes as her grip tightened on the knob of the door. "Yet you took the chance."

"You have to take chances. That's what life is all about." He smiled ruefully as he looked down at Davy. "But the dice were loaded against me this time. I'm really and truly hooked."

"You're in good company," she said huskily. "I'll take him now."

"You didn't sleep long."

"Enough." She came over to the rocking chair. "I think we'd better try weaning him from all this cuddling or none of us will get any sleep."

"Tomorrow." Jake reluctantly released Davy to her. "He's been sick."

"Tomorrow," she agreed indulgently.

He stood up. "I'll be back later."

She nodded as she watched him walk toward the door.

"Jake?"

He glanced back over his shoulder.

"We'll work something out. I know Davy needs a father."

"You're damn right. He also needs a mother. Does that suggest anything to you?"

He didn't wait for an answer before leaving the nursery, quietly closing the door behind him.

Kalana came into the nursery an hour later. The jeans and Bon Jovi sweatshirt she wore didn't disguise the slenderness of her figure, Mary noticed worriedly. "You've lost weight since Davy's been sick. Haven't you been eating?"

"Of course." Kalana's gaze slid away from Mary's. "I've only lost a few pounds. How is he?"

"Getting more spoiled by the minute." Mary grimaced. "But I promised Jake I'd give him one more day of it."

"Good." A smile lit Kalana's face. "I can't bear it when he cries." She asked hesitantly, "May I hold him?"

"Of course." Mary gave her the baby and stood up. "I've been meaning to apologize for being so sharp with you that first night. I was upset."

"I know." Kalana rocked Davy back and forth in her arms. "It's bad when babies are sick. They're so helpless." She looked at Mary over Davy's head. "But I think it's time I left your house."

"Why?" Mary asked, dismayed. "I told you I didn't mean to be—"

"That's not the reason. I just care too much for him," Kalana said simply. "It's dangerous to care too much when the child isn't your own."

"Dangerous? That's a rather dramatic word."

"Perhaps." Kalana lowered her gaze. "But the danger is there and I don't want to be hurt again. You should understand. You're also afraid of being hurt. You run away too."

Mary looked at her in surprise. "I'm not afraid."

"Yes, you are." Kalana shook her head. "I don't know why, but you're afraid of Jake. It seems very strange to me when he's been so good to you. There's so much hurt in the world that I'd think you'd be happy instead of afraid." She pressed her lips to the baby's silky brow. "I'll take him down to the kitchen while I fix his breakfast. Maybe a change of scene will perk up his appetite. Okay?"

"Okay." Mary watched Kalana carry Davy across the room toward the door. "Kalana."

Kalana looked back over her shoulder inquiringly.

"Don't leave us. Running away doesn't accomplish anything. Maybe we should both try to work through our problems and not bail out." Mary smiled warmly. "I don't have so many good friends that I can afford to do without you."

"You consider me your friend?"

"Of course." Mary looked at her in surprise. "Don't you think of me as a friend?"

"I was afraid to. . . ." Kalana stopped and shrugged. "You see what a coward I am? Friendship can be dangerous too." She smiled tremulously. "But I'll try, Mary."

"Me, too. You'll stay?"

Kalana hesitated. "You're sure?"

"Very sure."

Kalana smiled tentatively. "Then I'll stay for a while."

Mary's tone was firm. "A long while."

"It's bad luck to make plans for the future. It's safer to go day by day."

A thoughtful frown furrowed Mary's brow as she watched the door close behind Kalana.

Jake had said Mary was running away from him and she had resented the assertion. Yet Kalana had voiced the same idea.

She hadn't thought of herself as lacking in courage—but wasn't running away the mark of a coward?

Kalana was right: Jake had been good to her. No, not good: wonderful. He had gotten Davy and her out of Said Ababa, worked selflessly to straighten out that hideous red tape concerning her supposed death, given generously of his time and money. He had even cared enough to try to cure her of that damned phobia.

She had accepted it all as if it were her due, she realized with a shock.

In no way had Jake been at fault for her imprisonment. And getting pregnant had been as much her fault as Jake's. He really owed her nothing, and yet she had been selfishly accepting everything he had to give and returning nothing.

She shook her head in self-disgust as she slowly got to her feet. Good heavens, had she really believed she had such a monopoly on suffering that everyone else had to ease her way?

First, of course, she had to make sure Davy was returned to good health. But then she clearly had some serious thinking to do.

• • •

"I'd like to see Mr. Darcy." Mary tried to steady her breathing and look not at the crowds around her but at the man in the tuxedo by the door. He was a thin, dapper man with sharp eyes and unsmiling lips. She vaguely remembered seeing him the night she'd been at the casino before. "I'm Mrs. Darcy."

He straightened. "Good evening, Mrs. Darcy. I'm Bill Kenner. Jake's in his office. I'll have someone take you up."

"Just tell me where to go."

He looked hesitant. Mary could scarcely blame him, she thought ruefully. Everyone in the casino must have thought she was completely bananas the last time she was here. She smiled. "Really, I'll be fine."

He nodded at a bank of mirrored elevators across the foyer. "Third floor. I'll phone and tell—" He broke off as someone caught his eye across the foyer. "Bruno!"

Bruno stopped in midstride and turned toward them.

Kenner looked relieved. "Will you take Mrs. Darcy up to see Jake?"

"Sure. Hi, Mary. How's the kid?" Bruno ambled across the lobby and gently took her elbow. "Jake didn't tell me you were coming tonight."

"He doesn't know." Mary let him propel her across the lobby toward the elevators. It was a relief to have his big bulk running interference for her, but she was still glad to see the doors of the elevator close out the crowds. "It's a kind of surprise." She made a face. "Though I don't think Mr. Kenner believes Jake will appreciate it. He thinks I'm a loony."

"Bill's a good guy. He just knows Jake will have

his head if anything happens to you. He saw his face when you ran out of here that night." Bruno gave her a sober glance. "You do look a little nervous. You okay?"

"It's better than last time." She clutched her evening purse tightly. "Still not good."

"Next time it will be even better." Bruno smiled with surprising sweetness. "I'd lay odds on it."

The door opened and Bruno escorted her from the elevator across the corridor to a wide mahogany door. "I'm going to be up at the chalet Sunday. Jake's going to teach me to ski." He grimaced. "I was hoping he'd forget about it, but Jake never forgets." He knocked on the door and then opened it. "Company, Jake."

Jake looked up from the massive desk at the other end of the huge office and then stiffened in surprise. "Mary?"

"See you Sunday," Bruno said, pushing her gently into the office. He closed the door softly behind him.

"Hi." She took a deep breath and moved across the office toward the desk. "This is nice. I like it much better than the rest of the casino."

He stood up and came around the desk toward her. "I bet you do. No people. Why the hell didn't you tell me you were coming?"

"I wanted to do it on my own. Sort of a maiden voyage." She smiled. "Though I'm not a maiden, and for a minute downstairs I was afraid I might abandon ship."

"You should have called me. What if you'd panicked and run out in the street like you did last time? You're crazy."

"Mr. Kenner agrees with you." She moved forward

to stand directly in front of him. "I had to do it without you."

"Well, you did it." He added grimly, "Though I'll be damned if I let you go home without me."

"I don't intend to go home for a long time. I like it here." Mary looked around the huge office. Scarlet drapes veiled the large picture window across the room and couches and chairs in shades of creamy beige and ivory were scattered about the room. "This looks a little like the decor of the chalet."

"It was done by the same decorator." His gaze moved over her. "No red gown tonight."

"You said you liked the white lace better."

He went still. "And that mattered to you?"

"Yes." She forced herself to meet his gaze. "I like it better too. The red gown was bravado; this is me. I'm trying to be honest with both of us."

She could see the muscles of his shoulders bunching with tension beneath the smooth lines of his tuxedo jacket. "What the devil is that supposed to mean?"

"Is that the bathroom?" She nodded to a door to the left.

"Yes."

She moved toward the door. "Lock the hall door, Jake."

"What?"

"Lock the door, Jake." The bathroom door closed behind her and she leaned back against it. Her heart was beating harder than when she'd faced the crowds downstairs. She went to the basin and ran cold water over her wrists.

Five minutes later she opened the door and walked back into the office. She was wearing only the white, lacy, thigh-length slip she'd worn underneath her dress.

Jake was standing by the hall door, and he braced as if from a blow. "What's this supposed to be?"

"Seduction." Her voice was shaking a little. "I think. Though heaven knows I don't seem to be very good at it." She walked toward him, the thick-piled carpet springy beneath her bare feet. "You did it much better. I'd be more than willing to yield to you any time now."

"Here?" he asked hoarsely.

She nodded. "I was afraid, if it was too structured, I'd lose my nerve."

"We wouldn't want that." He took off his jacket and tossed it on the floor; his tie immediately followed. He went to the desk and picked up the receiver. "Hold my calls. I don't want to be disturbed."

She laughed huskily. "Won't they suspect what we're doing?"

"If they have any brains at all." His gaze ran slowly over her as he started to unbutton his shirt. "Would you mind them knowing?"

Her gaze centered in fascination on the dark triangle thatching his chest. "I'm not sure . . ."

"I don't mind. I like the idea that people might know." He was stripping more quickly. "Part of the primitive ego, I guess. Possession." He was naked and moved toward her. "No, obsession."

She had forgotten how overwhelming was the appeal of his tough, masculine beauty when naked. His maleness was overpowering: the tight buttocks and strong thighs, the full arousal. Now he was only a few inches from her, and she could feel the heat from his body, see his arousal, hear the quickened sound of his breathing. He hadn't touched her, and yet she felt as she had in the elevator so many years ago. Frantic. On fire.

He reached up and slowly pushed the thin straps of her slip from each shoulder.

She shivered as his fingers brushed against her flesh, sending fire streaking through her. He looked down at her breasts, barely covered by the silk bodice, and smiled. The smile was so sensuous she felt her chest tighten with the constriction of her breathing. "Pretty. Where did you get it?"

"What?"

"The slip. I like it." He pushed the slip down another inch.

"I don't remember." She couldn't remember her own name, she thought hazily. "Maybe Kalana—" She stopped speaking and inhaled sharply as he pushed the bodice down, totally baring her breasts.

He closed his eyes. "You should really try to remember. I'm sure we'll want to give them all our business." He took her hand and laid it palm down on his chest. His heart was thundering, his flesh hot to the touch. "And you'll need another slip quite soon."

"I will?"

He nodded, his eyes opening to look down at her. His hand closed on the bodice of the slip. "Quite soon." His hand suddenly moved forcefully downward, ripping the slip in two. "You see? Pity. But it got in the way of what we want." He tossed the slip aside and brought her into the cradle of his hips. "This *is* what we both want, isn't it, luv?"

The sudden barbarity of the action shocked and

stimulated her at the same time; the feel of him against her seared through Mary. "Yes," she whispered.

"Hold me," he muttered. He lifted her, sought, and plunged deep.

She cried out, clinging helplessly to him. "Jake!"

He didn't hear her; she doubted if he could hear anything as he lowered her to the floor. She could feel his heart thundering against her, and the look of painfully intense pleasure of his face was as arousing as his manhood within her.

The pile of the carpet beneath her was soft until he started to move, and then it was burning as erotically abrasive as was his manhood within her. He thrust frantically, urgently, arranging her to suit himself, murmuring inaudible words beneath his breath as he plunged.

Suddenly he stopped and was still, his manhood big, pulsing within her. He threw back his head, the tendons of his neck standing out, his jaw clenching. "Lord, it's too good. It's killing me."

It was killing her, too, she thought dazedly. She hadn't realized until now how high the sexual tension between them had built during the past months.

He looked down at her. "Too long . . ." He began to move again, fiercely, deeply.

Her head thrashed back and forth on the carpet as she surged upward, trying to take more of him, trying to give more. She heard herself moaning, gasping. Her nails dug into his shoulders as he lifted her to each thrust, lifted her to the quick and beyond. "Now, love." His voice was hoarse as he moved faster, harder. "Please, now."

She cried out as the tension exploded and he clutched her to him in a fiery series of spasms.

She couldn't catch her breath; she was too dizzy to see or hear. It had been too intense to bear and yet she found herself clinging to him, wanting the intensity to go on forever.

He was shuddering, holding her so tightly she couldn't get her breath.

"Jake, please."

He lifted his head and looked down at her, his chest rising and falling with his labored breathing. "I'm . . . sorry. I never seem to be able to take it slow and easy with you."

"I didn't ask you to be easy." She smiled tremulously. "But it would help if I could breathe."

His arms loosened but didn't let her go. "Why?"

"Because it's difficult to remain alive without breathing."

"You know what I mean." He moved off her and stood up. "Stay here." He strode across the office and into the bathroom. He returned in less than a minute with a large white bath towel in his hands. "Sit up."

She obediently sat up and he wrapped the towel around her, knotting it at her breasts. The towel barely skimmed her upper thighs.

"Is this supposed to keep me warm?" she asked, amused.

"No, it's supposed to keep you unoccupied for a few minutes." His gaze went to her thighs. "It may not succeed, but it's all the help we can get at the moment. If I'd known you were coming, I'd have had a robe here for you. I'll attend to that tomorrow." His glance lifted to her face. "You do know there's no going back, Mary? I can't go back to square one after this."

"If I remember, square one was a fairly intimate place to be." She brushed the hair back from her face and sat back on her heels. "Aren't you going to get something to cover yourself? It hardly seems fair to make—"

"Why?"

She met his gaze. "I realized I wasn't being fair to you," she said simply. "You've been very good to me, Jake. You were giving me everything and I was giving you nothing."

He went still. "So this is some kind of gift?"

"No." She smiled. "Well, if it was a gift, it was definitely mutual."

He smiled crookedly. "So I take it I'm not going to receive any declarations of undying devotion? This was sex, pure and simple?"

She gazed at him, troubled. "I can't change the way I feel. This is a big step for me. At first, I didn't think I could even do this. You make me feel too . . ." she shrugged helplessly. "It's too strong. I can't pledge any commitment."

"Because you're still frightened that I'll try to fence you in?" Jake's face tautened. "Dammit, don't you know that your shying away from me makes me want to do just that? I want you to stay with me because you want to be here. I've been trying to be patient, but I'm basically a primitive type, and when you run, I chase. It scares me to think you're edging away from me."

She looked down at herself, covered only with the towel. "I don't think this is edging away."

"It's a ray of hope." He gazed at her soberly. "But it's not enough."

"I can't give more now, Jake."

He nodded. "I know." He reached out and began to untie the knotted towel. "I'll take what I can get, but I don't guarantee I won't try for more. I'm desperate."

"What do you mean?"

The towel fell away from her and his head slowly lowered to her breasts. "I mean that there are all kinds of fences—some of them you never even dreamed existed, luv."

Eight

"You did very well, Bruno." Mary's eyes twinkled as she handed him one of the cups of chocolate on the tray. "There was a certain power and grace to—"

"Every fall I took," Bruno finished with a grimace. "I spent more time face down in the snow than Davy did." He sipped the chocolate and then looked contemplatively at the blazing logs in the fireplace. "But, you know, toward the end I kind of liked it. I didn't think I would."

She set the tray with Jake's hot chocolate on the coffee table. "Skiing is great fun." She took her own cup and saucer and sat down in the easy chair across from the couch where Bruno was sitting. "Why wouldn't you like it?"

"I like to be in control," Bruno said. "I *have* to be in control."

She looked down into the chocolate in her cup. "Then you must not have an easy time of it working for Jake."

"Sometimes we argue." He shrugged his massive shoulders. "But there are advantages too. You've got to weigh them against the cons."

"For instance?"

"I never had a close friend before I met Jake," Bruno said simply. "And there's no one more giving or loyal. That weighs pretty heavily with me." His gaze shifted to Mary's face. "You'll find it will be important to you, too, once you get over this jumpiness."

"It shows?"

"You tense up whenever he comes near you." He looked back at the fire. "I thought for a while it might be over, but it's not, is it? Give him a chance, Mary."

"Give him a chance?" Mary asked incredulously. "You don't know what you're talking about. He's not giving me a chance."

"He's moving into high gear?" Bruno nodded. "He can be pretty overpowering, but it's worth—"

"Davy's in the bath." Jake strode into the room, bringing with him a breezy vitality and exuberance that made Mary unconsciously stiffen in the chair. "Though I think Kalana is wetter than he is at the moment." He picked up his cup of hot chocolate from the tray and sat down on the arm of Mary's chair, idly swinging one jean-clad leg. "You'd think the kid would be exhausted after playing in the snow all afternoon."

"Well, this kid certainly is," Bruno said. "I'm glad I decided to spend the night. I'd probably fall asleep driving down the mountain."

"You'll get used to it." Jake's hand casually slid beneath the heavy fall of Mary's hair and began to knead the tendons of her nape. "After a few more lessons you'll be ready for the Olympics."

Mary felt her muscles tense and she carefully kept looking straight ahead. Jake's touch, though apparently casual, was infinitely sensual. He knew her nape was one of the most erogenous zones on her body, and he knew exactly what to do with his fingers there to arouse her. He should know, she thought with exasperation. He had spent the last four days acquiring perfect knowledge of her body—studying her reactions to every touch, every erotic stimulus, until he could make her almost feverish with desire with only an intimate look or a slight, but knowledgeable, touch. Since the night she had come to him at the casino, they hadn't left the chalet and had spent the greater part of their time there in bed.

He had concentrated all his attention on mastering her responses and he had succeeded damnably well. Even now, Mary's knowing he was deliberately arousing her didn't stop her breasts from swelling beneath her wool sweater.

Bruno's gaze became suddenly watchful. "I believe I'll skip the Olympics." He finished his chocolate and set the cup and saucer on the coffee table in front of him. "I'll go give Kalana a hand with Davy. We wouldn't want the kid to drown her."

"Tell Kalana dinner will be in an hour," Mary said.

"An hour and a half," Jake corrected. "I need time to rest. Teaching Bruno to ski is a drain on anyone's energy. I think hang gliding will be much easier."

"Hang gliding? I thought I'd talked myself out of that one. Not for a while, Jake. I need time to recuperate."

"Summer." Jake's thumbnail gently brushed back and forth on Mary's nape.

A hot shiver ran through her and she abruptly set her cup and saucer on the table beside her.

"The Alps are beautiful in the summer. It's an experience you shouldn't miss."

"We'll see." Bruno moved toward the door. "Maybe if you can show me a couple of stress tests on those blasted gliders. I'm no lightweight, remember."

He left the room and a moment later they heard his step on the stairs.

"I think he enjoyed himself today," Mary said.

"He's more open to new experiences than he likes to admit." Jake lifted her hair and lazily licked at her nape with catlike sensuality. "As you are, luv."

"I have to fix dinner."

"No, you don't. I'll do it. There's plenty of time." His hand moved down to caress her breasts, feeling the betraying swollen tautness. "Plenty of time. I've never made love to you in front of the fire. I understand it's *de rigueur*."

"Here?" Her gaze flew to his face. "But we can't. Bruno and Kalana . . ."

He set his cup on the table before leisurely pulling her sweater over her head and throwing it aside. "No one will come in. Bruno's no fool. He knew what was going on and he'll keep Kalana busy until dinner. I've been crazy to have you all afternoon." He began unbuttoning her blouse. "It must be all that fresh air."

"I . . . don't think fresh air has anything to do with it."

"You're probably right. I'm a sex maniac where you're concerned. Any time. Any place. . . ."

He pulled her up from the chair. "This place, Mary." He led her toward the fire, his voice coaxing. "The feel of the heat on your skin, the feel of me inside you. You know you'll like it." He pushed her to her knees on the rug before the fire and fell to his knees before her. "Slow and easy."

She met his gaze and saw the leaping flames of the fire reflected in his blue eyes.

She should resist. She knew what he was doing to her. He was conditioning her body to want him constantly, until to do without would be intolerable. Dear heaven, perhaps it had already happened.

Because she knew there was no way she could resist him at this moment.

She slowly lay down on the rug before the fire and looked up into his face, her gaze lingering on the wide, mobile mouth, the interesting planes of his jaw. Beautiful. Sensual and beautiful and . . . Jake.

"Slow and easy," she whispered.

"You're not talking to me," Jake said lightly as he buttoned her blouse. "Didn't I please you this time?"

"You know you did," Mary said wearily, not looking at him. "You make damn sure you do." She moved away from him and finished buttoning her blouse and then looked around for her sweater. She was still on her knees and crawled the few feet to where Jake had thrown it on the floor.

"Did I ever tell you how it turns me on to see how you fill out those jeans?"

She glanced over her shoulder to see Jake's gaze on her bottom.

"You have a world-class derriere, luv."

She pulled the sweater over her head and settled it around her hips. "Stop it, Jake."

"Oh, I have no intention of seducing you again. We've had our firelight. I can wait for bedtime." He smiled mischievously. "Maybe."

"I know what you're doing, you know."

He tucked his shirt into his jeans. "I thought you'd catch on. You're not stupid, luv. I just hoped I'd get enough momentum going before you found out what I was up to." He took a comb out of his pocket. "Your hair's all mussed. Come here and let me tidy it for you."

She stayed where she was, looking at him.

"You want me to come to you?" He stood up and crossed the intervening space in three strides. "No problem. I'm always willing to make the first move." He scooped her up in his arms and dropped into the easy chair with her on his lap.

"So I've noticed." She sat up straight, every muscle unyielding, as he began to run the comb through her hair. "And the second and the third."

"Sex?" He picked up a long strand of hair and examined it in the firelight. "You're getting sun-streaked from being outside so much. Isn't that pretty?"

"Yes, the sex."

"You won't give me anything else," he said. "It's all I've got to work with." He brushed her hair aside and kissed the sensitive cord of her neck. "Say you love me and I promise I won't touch you for at least two hours."

"Jake, dammit, I—"

"See? You won't admit it." He resumed combing her hair. "How can you expect me to give up the one weapon you've handed me if you won't give me something in exchange?"

She jumped off his lap and turned to face him. "You're not being fair, Jake."

He leaned back in the chair and gazed at her soberly. "Tell me you love me, Mary. Tell me you want to spend the rest of your life with me."

"I can't, Jake." Her hands clenched into fists at her sides. "It's too soon. You're crowding me. In your own way you're doing what Pallal did to me."

"The devil I am!"

"Yes, you are. It's conditioning. Calculated conditioning. Only with Pallal it was fear."

His hands clenched on the arms of his chair. "I can see you slipping away from me, and it's my worst nightmare. Hell, yes, I try to make you dependent on me for sex. And I'll keep on doing it." He paused. "Until you could no more think of leaving me than I could of leaving you."

She backed away from him. "It won't be so easy after tomorrow."

He tensed, his gaze narrowing on her face. "No?"

"I'm starting lessons in St. Moritz." She turned and walked over to stand before the fireplace and look into the fire. "I'll be gone most of the day and some evenings."

"What kind of lessons?"

"Jewelry design. It's what I've always wanted to do."

"I remember." Jake was silent for a few minutes. "Clever move, luv. You know I'd never try to stop you from doing something you'd been cheated of during those years." He laughed mirthlessly. "I suppose I should be grateful you're so frantic to get away from me that you're willing to brave the crowds in town. Everything has an up side, doesn't it?"

"I have to start making a life for myself. You've seen everything and done everything, Jake." Her voice was suddenly urgent. "My life was put on hold."

"Do you think I don't know that? Do you think I don't want to see you happy and fulfilled? My Lord, don't you know—" He broke off and got to his feet. "Okay, I'll arrange for a car to take you into St. Moritz and bring you back. I trust you're still planning on staying at the chalet?"

"If you still want me to stay here."

"Oh yes, I want you," he said thickly. "In my house. In my bed. I'm not giving up just because you've thrown a monkey wrench into the works. If I can't have the main course, I'll take the leftovers." He turned and moved toward the door. "I'll just have to make sure the leftovers are more appetizing for you than the dinner itself. Speaking of dinner, please turn on the broiler, luv. I'll be down in a minute to put on the steaks. I just want to tuck Davy into bed."

She gazed after him with tears in her eyes. Jake was everything any woman could wish for in a man: tender, passionate, caring. If he had been less possessive and dominating she might have been able to give him what he wanted. But he could no more change his character than she could her own. He would always seek to protect and dominate and she would always flinch from that aspect of his character. The sad thing about the whole mess was that Jake understood this about her, as he did everything else, and yet could not stop himself from trying to keep her in his velvet-lined prison.

Yes, she was being very wise to draw away and put some space between them.

Yet that wisdom didn't make her less lonely in this moment.

Nor did it cause the pain to go away when she remembered the expression on Jake's face as he had left the room.

"You're doing that christie turn with all the grace of a pregnant water buffalo," Jake said as Bruno skied up to the pickup truck on the road bordering the slope. "You're getting cocky."

"I was in a hurry to get down the slope." Bruno grinned as he pushed up his goggles. "I've decided that momentum, not skill, is the goal."

"You'll 'momentum' yourself into an abyss one of these days, if you don't learn a few skills to go along with it." Jake took off his own skis and tossed them into the back of the pickup truck. "Come on. You've had enough for today."

"One more run. I'm just getting started." Bruno's dark eyes sparkled. "You can go on, if you like. I can get to the chalet on my own."

"I think I've created a monster." Jake levered himself up onto the bed of the pickup truck. "Okay, one more run. I'll wait." His lips twisted. "I haven't anything more important to do."

Bruno's grin faded. "Mary's at school?"

"Mary's always at school or at a seminar or playing with Davy or—" He broke off and shrugged. "You get the picture."

"It's been only three weeks, Jake. She'll get bored with it."

"I don't *want* her to get bored," Jake said with sudden violence. "I want her to love every minute of the work she's doing. I just want to share it with her. I want to have her talk to me about it and—Bruno, I don't want her to shut me out of her life."

"Jake, Mary does care about you." Bruno frowned. "Maybe she only needs the time away from you."

"I know she cares. And I know I was a damn fool for trying to tie her down. I can't seem to do anything right where Mary's concerned." He made an impatient gesture with his left hand. "Go take your last run. I want to get back to the chalet and make some phone calls."

"Urgent?"

"No, I don't think so." Jake gazed thoughtfully at the skis on the truck next to him. "I had a report from Hassan and I want to verify it."

"The call's to Said Ababa?"

Jake nodded. "It's probably nothing, but it never hurts to make sure."

The abstracted frown still furrowed Jake's brow as he watched Bruno turn away and start up the slope for his last run.

"I don't want you going into St. Moritz for a few days," Jake said quietly as he came out of the bathroom wearing only a towel about his hips. "I've told the driver he won't be needed until further notice."

Mary stiffened on the vanity bench. "What?"

"I think you heard me. I can practically feel you bristling from here."

"Why?"

"Not because I want to keep you prisoner on my

mountaintop. Oh, I do. But that's not the reason."
He took the towel off and moved toward the bed
across the room. "It's just a security measure."

"What kind of security measure?" she asked warily.

"Come to bed." He slid beneath the covers and
patted the silken counterpane. "And take that bloody
nightgown off. You know you won't need it. Bed is
the one place we're always in complete agreement."

She stood up and walked toward him. "Why
shouldn't I go to St. Moritz? I have tests this week."

"Make them up later."

She sat down on the side of the bed. "Why, Jake?"

"Pallal."

She went rigid, fear icing down her spine.

"It may be nothing, but Hassan called me yesterday and told me that Pallal had boarded an international flight."

"For here?"

"Hassan couldn't determine the destination."

"But you think—"

"I don't think anything. I want to be careful. I've
set guards around the chalet and I don't want you
leaving it until I find out where Pallal surfaces."

She laid down and pulled the covers over her.
"No."

He stiffened beside her. "No?"

"I won't let Pallal make a prisoner out of me again,"
she said fiercely. "Do you know what my first instinct was when you mentioned his name? To hide
away, to find a cave somewhere and hide in the
darkness. Well, I won't do it. I won't hide away simply because I hear Pallal has decided to get on an
airplane. Can't you see? If I did, he'd be able to keep
me his captive for the rest of my life."

Jake was silent a moment. "Yes, I can see. I wish to hell I couldn't."

"Keep the guards around the chalet. I want Davy safe." She shivered. "And I wouldn't mind a guard or two watching me either. I'm scared, Jake."

"But not scared enough to give in to him." His lips feathered her temple as he drew her into his arms. "That's what's important, Mary. Not the fear, but the facing it."

She laughed softly. "Like you faced your Zulus who wanted to peg you out for the ants?"

"Not like that at all," he said. "Did I ever tell you about the KGB and the radar installation plans?"

He was trying to distract her again, she thought with a sudden surge of tenderness. He had accepted her fear as well as her determination and was trying to help her with both. "No, you never got around to it."

"How remiss of me. Well, I was in Moscow on a bit of less than legal business when who should come prancing up to me but this Russian major who turned out to be as larcenous as . . ." His voice droned on while his hand gently stroked her hair.

Mary paid little attention to the words, but she gradually began to relax, and before the story was half finished the fear gripping her had withdrawn into the shadows.

But not so the tenderness. The tenderness expanded and grew until it seemed to fill the world. Shining, radiant and without end.

"Mary, are you asleep?"

"No." she raised herself on one elbow to gaze down at him. "I was just thinking what a magnificent liar you are."

"Anything worth doing, is worth doing well." His gaze searched her face. "Is that all you were thinking?"

"Not bloody likely," she said, gently mimicking his faint cockney accent. "I was thinking I'd forgotten to take off this blasted nightgown."

She pulled the gown over her head and threw it across the room. "And I was wondering if I could persuade you to forget the KGB and the Zulus for enough time to—"

His lips cut off the rest of her words as he pulled her back down into his arms.

Nine

"I'll be here to pick you up at three." Jake leaned across her and opened the passenger door. "Don't worry. You'll be watched every minute. I have security men inside keeping an eye on the corridors and the classrooms."

She tried to smile. "We're going to feel awfully foolish if Pallal doesn't show up here."

"I wouldn't mind egg on my face if it means keeping you safe." Jake kissed her on the cheek and gave her a nudge. "Get going. I want to see you inside before I radio our contact you're on your way."

"You'll be careful? After all, you're the one Pallal hates." Her lips twisted. "He only looked on me as a victim."

"Then he's an idiot. There's no way you're a victim any longer." Jake grinned. "And neither am I."

Mary got out of the car, her boots crunching into the ice-encrusted snow at the curb. "Three o'clock." She slammed the door shut and walked briskly up

the sidewalk to the old nineteenth-century brown-
stone that housed the school.

It was probably idiotic to be this nervous. What
could Pallal do here in St. Moritz? He held power in
Said Ababa, but not anywhere else in the world.
Jake must possess more power and connections than
Pallal. Everything would be all right, she told her-
self. They would all go on with their lives and if
Pallal appeared on the scene they would deal with
him.

In spite of the reassurance she was striving to
instill in herself, she still felt distinctly uneasy as
she opened the door of the front entrance and entered the school.

She would be very glad when three o'clock came
and she could be with Jake again.

Jake didn't pick her up at three o'clock as he had
promised.

Mary felt her heart lurch when she saw that it was
Bruno at the wheel of the Mercedes as it pulled up
in front of the school. "Get in, Mary."

"Where's Jake?" Mary opened the door and got
into the passenger seat, her gaze searching Bruno's
face. "Something's happened, hasn't it?" She could
feel the panic rising within her. "Where the hell is
Jake?"

"Pallal."

Mary closed her eyes. "He's dead, isn't he? Jake's
dead."

"No." Bruno's tone was gentle. "He's not dead and,
with any luck, he's not going to be."

"Pallal has him?"

"No." Bruno hesitated. "He's got Davy."

Mary's eyes flew open. "Dear God, how? Jake ringed the chalet with guards. No one could have gotten through them."

"No one got into the chalet." Bruno's lips tightened grimly. "Just before noon Kalana came running out of the chalet carrying Davy. She told Werner, the security chief, she had to get the kid to a doctor. Werner followed her down the mountain. She was going fast, and they were having a hard time keeping her in sight on those twisting curves. About two miles from the chalet they came around a turn and found the road blocked by a fallen tree and Pallal on the other side."

"Davy's sick again?" Mary had been stopped short by that one sentence. "And Pallal has him?"

Bruno shook his head. "Werner said Kalana obviously expected to be intercepted. She climbed over the fallen tree, ran over to Pallal's car, and jumped into the passenger seat." He paused. "She handed Davy to Pallal on a silver platter."

"No, you're wrong. She wouldn't do that." Mary shook her head dazedly. "She loves Davy. She'd never hurt him."

"I didn't think so either. I liked the girl." Bruno's expression hardened. "But she sure as hell did it, Mary."

"Why?" The tears brimmed Mary's eyes. "It doesn't make sense."

"Who the hell knows why anyone turns Judas?" Bruno asked wearily. "It's done and Pallal has Davy. And he'll soon have Jake."

"Jake! You said Jake was safe."

"For now. Pallal phoned Jake at the casino. He wants ransom for Davy. He wants all the cash in the casino safe and he said he'd let Kalana take Davy back to the chalet if Jake would take the boy's place."

"And Jake's going to do it." It was a statement. Of course Jake would do it. Jake loved Davy as much as she did.

"He just left the casino. He's on his way to the chalet where Pallal's holding Davy now. Jake's supposed to leave his car around the turn of the road about a mile from the chalet, and as soon as Pallal sees Jake walking toward the chalet, he'll send Kalana and the kid out and Kalana can drive Jake's car home."

"Very efficient. Like some kind of spy exchange," Mary said numbly. "But he's still going to kill Jake."

"Not if I can help it. I'm going after him. It shouldn't be too difficult. Werner said Pallal only had one other man in the car. He's not on his home turf and he doesn't have his legions to call on. I'll follow Jake to the chalet with a few men and see if we can take them both."

"And what about Jake?" Mary asked fiercely. "Pallal will have a gun and they won't let Jake within ten feet of the chalet if he's armed. You try to free him and they'll shoot Jake."

"Jake's been in tight corners before. Maybe it—"

"*Maybe?* Do you think I'm going to let Pallal kill Jake?" she asked. "Take me to the casino. Hurry."

Hearing the urgency in her voice, Bruno instinctively stepped on the accelerator. "Why?"

"The Burgundy Princess. Pallal has always wanted

it. He even killed my father to get it. Jake told me he put it in the safe at the casino, and he gave me the combination." She moistened her lips with her tongue. "I just hope he wants it more than he wants Jake dead."

Bruno's eyes narrowed thoughtfully. "It might work. At least, it's more than we had before."

"But why the devil didn't Jake take the Princess? He could have worked an exchange for Davy with the necklace instead of putting his own head on the block."

Bruno said quietly, "Maybe he didn't feel it was his to take. The Princess is your property and you've made damn sure Jake knows you don't want to belong to him in any way that matters."

She stared at him, stunned. He was right. She had never given Jake any assurance that would have prevented him from going blindly into Pallal's trap. The Princess was the only personal wealth she had left and it was to have been her ticket to independence. Jake would have believed he had no right to rob her of it, even if it meant risking his own life. If Jake died, it would be her fault.

But Jake wasn't going to die. She wouldn't let him die. "Can you get me to Pallal's chalet right away?"

"I'll do my damndest." Bruno paused. "But it may be too late."

Fear clutched her throat and for a moment she couldn't speak. "I don't think so. Not if you get me there within a few minutes of Jake's arrival at the chalet. Pallal's very deliberate. He likes to take his time about getting his pound of flesh."

The car pulled up in front of the casino and the

doorman opened the passenger door. "I'll be right back. Keep the motor running." She stepped out of the car and hurried toward the door of the casino.

The small chalet squatted perilously on the side of the mountain, with only a stand of pine trees on one side and on the other the long verge sloping steeply to the valley below. Bruno screeched to a stop directly in back of Jake's Mercedes. Mary jumped out of the car before it had come to a full stop. "Stay here."

"The hell I will," Bruno said roughly. "Do you think I'm going to let you handle this alone?"

"Yes, because it's our only chance." Mary strode quickly toward the curve of the road. "Don't argue with me, Bruno. Pallal sees me as no threat. But if you show up, Jake's dead."

She turned the corner of the road, her gaze flying to the door of the chalet. She felt suddenly limp with relief. Jake was just disappearing through the doorway of the chalet. She caught only the fleetest glimpse of the back of his black windbreaker, but there was no one else who walked with that springy, loose-limbed grace. He was still alive.

"Mary?"

Kalana was walking toward her and was now only a few feet away. She carried Davy in her arms. The exchange had been made.

Kalana stopped short, her eyes widening. "No, go back."

"Is Davy all right?"

Kalana nodded. "You know I'd never let anything happen to him."

"Do I?" Mary took a step forward. "Bruno's waiting in the car. Take Davy and get out of here, Kalana." She tried to keep her voice from shaking with anger. "Though I don't expect Bruno to give you a very gentle welcome. He loves Jake."

"I didn't expect anything else." Kalana's pinched face glimmered as pale as the snow around them. "I knew you'd hate me." She drew a shaky breath. "Don't do it. Pallal will be watching, and he's very angry with you for tricking him."

"I have something to sweeten his temper." Mary gestured with her hand. "I can't waste any more time. Get out of here."

Kalana's arms tightened around Davy and she hurried past Mary toward the turn of the road. "I'm sorry, Mary. I couldn't help it. I couldn't let him . . ." Kalana's words trailed away as she disappeared beyond the turn of the road.

Mary hurried to take cover in the thick stand of pine trees bordering the edge of the mountain. "Pallal," she called. "Come out here!"

"Why should I?" Pallal asked. "Really, Mary, you've been very foolish. You can't possibly hope to free Darcy. Be content. I've given you back your son." He paused. "For the time being."

"I have a bargain for you."

"I've made my bargain for the day. I have a considerable amount of cash and Jake Darcy."

"But you don't have the Burgundy Princess."

Pallal was silent for a few moments.

"And do you?"

"I have it around my neck."

"Step out so that I can see it."

"Don't do it, Mary," Jake shouted.

"You'll see it when we make our deal. It's very beautiful, Pallal. You have always wanted it, haven't you? Isn't it worth Jake's life?"

"Throw it out in the snow."

"If you'll bring Jake out here and let him go."

Another silence.

"I don't think so. Darcy has annoyed me. And all I have to do is to send my man after you to take the necklace."

"No, you can't. Because the minute you do, I'll throw the Princess over the cliff."

"You wouldn't do that. You might never find it again. It's worth millions."

"Try me. You've wanted the Princess too long to lose it now. Bring Jake out and let him come to me."

"All right, it's a deal." Pallal appeared in the doorway and smiled mockingly. "We'll let you and Darcy run for it. I haven't had any good hunting for a long time."

"Bring him out."

Jake suddenly appeared in the doorway, a rivulet of blood running from the corner of his mouth. "Mary, for God's sake, this is crazy. You're crazy."

"Did he hurt you?"

"No, but—"

Pallal pushed Jake forward with the barrel of his gun. "Let's get on with it. Do be aware I have a man in the cabin with a rifle pointed at you."

Mary watched them come toward her. When they were within a hundred yards she said sharply, "Stop. Now let him come the rest of the way alone."

Pallal hesitated. "Go on, Darcy. Mary, throw out the necklace."

Jake moved quickly forward.

"The necklace," Pallal said. "Hurry or I'll put a bullet in his back."

The moment she threw him the necklace, he would snatch it up and immediately shoot Jake. She stepped out of the shelter of the pines and took off the necklace, letting Pallal see the rich glittering of the diamonds and ruby.

His gaze hungrily fastened on the necklace. "My God, you *do* have it. I was afraid it was a bluff."

"I don't bluff with my husband's life."

Jake was within fifty yards of the pines now. She held out the necklace. "You could have had it any time when I was in Balahar. You had all the weapons."

"I'll have it now. Throw it!"

He was becoming suspicious.

"Run, Jake!"

Mary hurled the necklace with all her might toward the snowy verge sloping down to the valley. The Princess soared past Pallal in a sparkling arc to land on the upper slope. It immediately began to slide down the mountain.

Pallal screamed a curse and dove after it.

Jake bolted across the clearing and reached Mary in seconds.

"Mary, are you trying to give me a heart attack?" He grabbed her arm and was running with her through the trees. She heard Pallal shout and felt a rifle bullet whiz past her ear.

Jake pushed her behind a tree and drew a pistol from beneath the windbreaker.

Mary's eyes widened. "Where did you get the gun?"

"Kalana. She slipped it to me when we passed

during the exchange." Jake was sighting carefully. "But it doesn't have the range of that rifle Pallal's buddy is using. I'll have to wait . . ." He fired the gun and then smiled grimly. "But it shoots straight. One down and—"

A shot broke the stillness.

A shrill scream echoed on the cold air.

"That was Pallal," Mary whispered. "Bruno?"

Another shot and then another.

Mary pushed closer to Jake, her gaze on the arrested expression on Jake's face. "What's happening?"

"Kalana."

Another shot.

"Come on. I think it's over." Jake took Mary's arm and propelled her out into the open.

Near the chalet she could see a man in an orange ski suit lying in the snow, his rifle beside him. But it was the figures only a few yards away from them that held her attention.

Kalana stood over Pallal, a pistol still smoking in her hand.

Pallal's eyes were open, staring sightlessly into the sky.

"He's dead." Jake gently took the pistol from Kalana. "You won't need this anymore."

"No, it's over now," Kalana said dully. "Four shots. One for each of them."

"Each?" Mary asked.

"My family. My mother, my father, my sister." Kalana paused. "My brother. He killed them all. They were all at Balahar. I knew about the others, but I thought he'd spared my little brother." Her expression was suddenly anguished. "Delan was only four. I didn't see how anyone could kill a little boy. Pallal said if I'd do everything he told me to do my brother would live. That's when he gave me Davy to care for. When Jake came to the village I knew I had to go with him in case Pallal wanted something more from me." She turned to Mary. "I didn't want to do it. I . . . I like you."

"Pallal called you and gave you orders to bring Davy to him?"

"I knew he'd ask it of me someday. When I first came here Jake had me do all the shopping and I bought two guns. I wasn't sure what I'd do with them, but I knew I couldn't let Pallal hurt Davy. Then, when he called me, I brought both guns with me. One for me and one for Jake." Her voice broke. "Pallal said he'd brought my brother and would free him if I gave him Davy." The tears began to run down her face. "It was a lie. He told me after I reached here that my brother had died in Balahar."

Mary reached out and gently touched her arm. "I'm sorry, Kalana."

Kalana jerked her arm away. "Why are you being so kind to me? I *betrayed* you."

"For God's sake, I know how far anyone would go to save a child," Mary said. "If anything had happened to Jake or Davy I would have strangled you myself, but I can understand why you did it. I would have done anything to get Davy away from Pallal."

"I killed him. You're supposed to feel bad when you take a life." Kalana looked down at Pallal. "But I don't feel anything."

"You will later." Jake took her arm and gently led

her away from Pallal's body. "Though I hope not much. Pallal's not worth it."

"Where's Davy, Kalana?" Mary asked.

"I left him with Bruno."

"Bruno let you come back here?" Mary looked at the turn of the road and saw Bruno striding toward them across the clearing, Davy in his arms.

"Of course." Kalana smiled without mirth. "He knew I'd betrayed you. He wouldn't care if I chose to kill myself. Bruno doesn't like traitors." Her smile vanished. "Neither do I."

"Come on, let's get back to the chalet." Mary put her arm around Kalana. "You're shaking."

"No, don't touch me. Don't be kind to me," Kalana sobbed. "Can't you see? I shouldn't have . . . but I didn't know what else I could do." Kalana turned and started to run, stumbling over the rough clumps of ice and snow.

"Jake, we've got to catch her," Mary said. "Help her."

"Not now. We're the worst possible people to help her now."

"But she's so alone."

"Later. She has to come to terms with her guilt by herself."

"Guilt? She couldn't help herself."

"That doesn't alter her guilt." Jake put his arm around Mary's shoulders. "Come on, let's get Davy home. I'll send Bruno after Kalana. She won't get far in the shape she's in right now."

"She said Bruno hated traitors."

"But she'll be better able to face his coldness than our forgiveness."

Mary hesitated, looking after Kalana's retreating figure before turning away. "Very well," she said wearly. "Let's go home, Jake."

Bruno brought Kalana back to the chalet three hours after Jake and Mary had arrived.

Kalana was still pale, but dry-eyed and composed. "I'm going away. I'll just pack a suitcase and then—"

"Don't be ridiculous," Mary said. "We want you to stay."

"And I want to stay," Kalana said in a low voice. "But I've done a great wrong and I must be punished. Bruno and I are very much alike." She glanced at Bruno, who was standing with an impassive face by the front door. "We both believe disloyalty should be punished. You won't do it, so I must do it myself. The greatest punishment I can think of is to leave Davy." She started up the stairs. "Bruno is taking me to the bus station. I'll be—"

"Where are you going?" Jake asked.

"I'm not sure." She glanced over her shoulder. "But you mustn't worry about me. I've taken care of myself for a long time. I'll find work."

"Let us help until—"

"No!" Kalana tempered the sharpness of her tone with the next words. "No help. May I say good-bye to Davy?"

"Of course." Mary could feel her throat tighten helplessly. "Come back to us, Kalana."

"Perhaps, someday." Kalana smiled tremulously. "I'm truly not running away this time, Mary. I'm done with running."

"So am I," Mary said.

Kalana glanced from Mary's face to Jake's and nodded slowly. "I see that you have." She turned and started back up the stairs to say her good-bye to Davy.

Thirty minutes later Kalana left the chalet and drove down the mountain with Bruno toward St. Moritz.

Ten

"Go to bed." Jake kissed Mary's cheek and gave her a gentle nudge toward the stairs. "You're so exhausted you're about to keel over."

She did feel tired, she thought. Tired and discouraged and sad. Why did there have to be children like Kalana in the world who could be victimized by scum like Pallal? Kalana should be going to dances and having her first case of puppy love, and instead the girl was on a bus going toward still more insecurity.

"She'll be fine," Jake said, as if reading her mind. "She's tough. I'll have Bruno keep an eye on her once she gets settled."

"She shouldn't have to be tough. She's still a child herself." Mary turned away and moved toward the stairs. "Coming?"

He shook his head. "I have a few grueling hours to go through with the local police. There are two bodies to account for."

"Will there be a problem?"

"I doubt it. The local government has had trouble with Swiss nationals being ill-treated by Said Ababa." He smiled wryly. "They may want to give Kalana a medal."

Mary felt a surge of relief. "That's good. All Kalana would need is a murder charge hanging over her to totally ruin her life."

"I'll work it out." He strode toward the front door. "Go to bed and get some rest. Don't worry about anything. Leave it all to me."

The front door closed behind him before she could reply.

Mary trudged slowly up the stairs, thinking about his words.

Leave it all to Jake.

Jake was taking charge, smoothing her path again, taking the brunt of her problems on his shoulders. Once more he was sheltering her, enclosing her in that protective box.

Why did she feel neither resentful nor threatened? She felt only warmth and gratitude and something infinitely deeper. The change of attitude held a significance that was of the utmost importance, and she knew she had to talk to Jake.

But Jake wasn't there, and she was so numbed and weary from the events of the day that she could scarcely put two thoughts together, much less put them into words.

She would take a nap and talk to Jake when he came home.

Jake was not in bed next to Mary when she awoke at quarter to four the following morning.

The knowledge immediately jarred her wide-awake, and in seconds she was out of bed and pulling on her robe.

What if that business with the police had not gone as well as Jake believed it would? He was well thought of in both municipal and diplomatic circles, but there was no question his past was distinctly questionable.

She turned on the lamp and picked up the receiver of the phone on the bedside table. She dialed Bruno's number in St. Moritz and it was picked up after three rings.

"Bruno, Jake's not here," she said, not giving him a chance to say more than hello. "The police have arrested him. I knew I shouldn't have let him go without—"

"Easy, Mary." Bruno's voice was soothing. "The police released Jake two hours ago. The case is closed."

Her anxiety ebbed but failed to recede entirely. "Then why isn't he home?"

"He said he was going back to Pallal's chalet to look for the Burgundy Princess."

Dear heaven, she had completely forgotten about the necklace. She had a sudden memory of the glittering jewels sliding down the snowy mountainside. "It's still dark out, for Pete's sake. He can't even see."

"He said he has to find it."

"He'll fall off the damn mountain."

Bruno chuckled. "He's pretty surefooted."

"He's no mountaineer. Why didn't you go with him?"

"He said he could handle it himself."

"Leave it all to Jake?"

"What?"

"Nothing," Mary said. "Bruno, could you come and take care of Davy?"

"You're going after Jake?"

"You bet I am. I have to shower and dress, but that shouldn't take long. Can you be here in thirty minutes?"

"Why not? Who needs sleep anyway?"

"I'll make it up to you."

"Just make it up to Jake."

"I will," she whispered. "I promise, Bruno."

She replaced the receiver and hurried into the bathroom.

The mountaineer's rope was tied around the bole of the pine tree closest to the sloping verge and pulled taut, disappearing over the edge.

"Jake!" Mary shined her flashlight down the mountain, following the rope down the slippery, glistening white terrain. Dear heaven, she couldn't see him. What if he'd fallen or the rope had caught and he was hanging helplessly. "Jake, dammit, you come up here!"

"Mary?"

She stepped closer to the edge of the cliff and shined her flashlight deeper into the ravine. The beam fell on Jake's close-cropped black hair and she felt almost weak with relief. "Who else would be crazy enough to follow you out here in the middle of the night? Come up here or I'll come down."

"Stay there! I'll come right up."

She stepped back from the edge of the mountain and waited impatiently for him to work his way up the ice-covered slope. Dawn was breaking but the early light was gray, bleak. The air was frigid, even colder than yesterday, and her breath formed misty clouds on the still air.

It took Jake a good five minutes before he reached the top of the incline. He was wearing a vest harness of leather over his jacket, she noticed with relief. At least he hadn't been banking entirely on his grip on that slender rope. But, as usual, he wasn't wearing either a hat or gloves, and it was very cold.

She reached out and grabbed his arm and pulled him the last few feet. "You couldn't wait for daylight? You couldn't ask for help from Bruno? You couldn't ask help from me?"

He shined his flashlight on her face. "You're angry."

"I'm mad as hell. It's not enough that you scare me half to death yesterday by marching into Pallal's hands like the proverbial sacrificial lamb. Now you have to play mountain climber in the middle of the night to retrieve that blasted necklace."

"I was afraid it would slip farther down the mountain and we wouldn't be able to find it."

"I don't care if it falls to China. It's not worth you getting your neck broken or—"

He chuckled. "I agree about the broken neck, but the Princess is worth a mild case of frostbite."

"This isn't funny."

Jake's grin faded. "The Princess belongs to you, Mary. You threw it away to save my life, but I couldn't let you lose it."

"I threw it away because it didn't matter two cents compared to keeping you alive." Her eyes glittered with tears. "*You're* what's important to me."

He went still. "Would you care to elaborate?"

"I don't care about my freedom or my indepen-dence or . . . Well, I do, but I can handle you being domineering. I may even try a little domination my-self, if you ever do anything as foolish as this again."

"Mary, slowly and clearly."

Mary drew a deep breath. "I love you, Jake. I've loved you since the minute I looked at you at that tea dance three years ago, and I'll love you forever and ever. Is that clear enough?"

A radiant smile lit his face. "That will do quite well, thank you." His hands were quickly untying the rope from around his middle. "You do pick your moments, when I'm trussed-up like this. Feel free to continue your declaration while I get out of this harness."

"I realized yesterday when I was so afraid Pallal would kill you that all the freedom in the world wouldn't make me happy if you weren't there to share it. I wanted to kill you for not taking the Princess and bargaining for your life."

"You mean I actually have Pallal to thank for some-thing?" He pulled the harness off and threw it on the ground. "You know, I kind of suspected you'd discovered a fondness for me when you threw the Princess into the wild blue yonder. I've never had anyone toss their security and freedom down a moun-tainside to save my skin. It was most gratifying." He took a step closer and framed her face in his two hands. His palms were cold and hard and the emo-tion shining in his eyes was radiant. "Now say it again."

"I love you." She smiled as she mimicked huskily, "In fact, you're the bloody center of my existence, mate. I don't know why you've been so patient with me, but—"

He kissed her gently, sweetly, and the morning was no longer either bleak or frigid.

"You're touched in the head, luv. I love you so much I couldn't do anything right. We both know I made so many mistakes I almost blew it."

"Me, too." She went into his arms and held him tightly. "But maybe we had too much, too soon. Maybe your blasted destiny decided to back up and make us start over so that we'd appreciate what we had." She frowned fiercely. "Perhaps I can accept that you thought I was so selfish I'd keep the Princess and let you ransom Davy with your hide, but coming out here in the middle of the night is going a little too far. Don't you ever do anything like this again without telling me."

"I had to get the Princess."

"Damn the Princess."

"You don't want it?" He pushed her back to look down at her. He thrust his hand into the pocket of his windbreaker and pulled out the necklace. "Should I toss it back into the snowy depths?"

The first light of dawn caught the rich splendor of the ruby and turned the diamond chain into an effulgence of rainbow prisms.

"You found it." She looked at the necklace and then smiled up at him. "Let's save it for Davy. I think every family should have heirlooms to bestow, don't you?"

"For Davy," he repeated, cramming the Burgundy Princess back into his pocket. He put his arm around her waist and began to lead her away from the snow-covered verge toward the road. "Let's go tell him about it."

"I doubt if he'll understand. His vocabulary isn't extensive, you know."

"Are you putting down my son? I'll have you know he called me Daddy day before yesterday." His brow wrinkled thoughtfully. "But maybe you're right. Since he can't verbalize very well yet perhaps I should teach him a few pithy quotes to stun the populace."

"For instance?"

"Why, luv, I thought you'd surely guess. What else?" Jake's eyes twinkled as his lips feathered her ear in the most loving of caresses. "All's well that ends well."

THE EDITOR'S CORNER

This month our color reflects the copper leaves of autumn, and we hope when a chill wind blows, you'll curl up with a LOVESWEPT. In keeping with the seasons, next month our color will be the deep green of a Christmas pine, and our books will carry a personalized holiday message from the authors. You'll want to collect all six books just because they're beautiful—but the stories are so wonderful, even wrapped in plain brown paper they'd be appealing!

Sandra Brown is a phenomenon! She never disappoints us. In **A WHOLE NEW LIGHT**, LOVESWEPT #366, Sandra brings together two special people. Cyn McCall desperately wants to shake up her life, but when Worth Lansing asks her to spend the weekend with him in Acapulco, she's more than a little surprised—and tempted. Worth had always been her buddy, her friend, her late husband's business partner. But what will happen when Cyn sees him in a whole new light?

Linda Cajio's gift to you is a steamy, sensual romance: **UNFORGETTABLE,** LOVESWEPT #367. Anne Kitteridge and James Farraday also know each other. In fact, they've known each other all their lives. Anne can't forget how she'd once made a fool of herself over James. And James finds himself drawn once again to the woman who was his obsession. When James stables his prize horse at Anne's breeding farm, they come together under the most disturbingly intimate conditions, and there's no way they can deny their feelings. As always Linda creates an emotionally charged atmosphere in this unforgettable romance.

(continued)

Courtney Henke's first LOVESWEPT, **CHA-MELEON,** was charming, evocative, and tenderly written, and her second, **THE DRAGON'S REVENGE,** LOVESWEPT #368 is even more so. J.D. Smith is instantly captivated by Charly, the woman he sees coaching a football team of tough youths, and he wonders what it would be like to tangle with the woman her players call the Dragon Lady. He's met his match in Charly—in more ways than one. When he teaches her to fence, they add new meaning to the word touché.

Joan Elliott Pickart will cast a spell over you with **THE MAGIC OF THE MOON,** LOVESWEPT #369. She brings together Declan Harris, a stressed-out architect, and Joy Barlow, a psychologist, under the rare, romantic light of a blue moon—and love takes over. Declan cherishes Joy, but above all else she wants his respect—the one thing he finds hardest to give. Joan comes through once more with a winning romance.

LOVESWEPT #370, **POOR EMILY** by Mary Kay McComas is not to be missed. The one scene sure to make you laugh out loud is when Emily's cousin explains to her how finding a man is like choosing wallpaper. It's a scream! Mary Kay has a special touch when it comes to creating two characters who are meant to be together. Emily falls for Noble, the hero, even before she meets him, by watching him jog by her house every day. But when they do meet, Emily and Noble find they have lots more in common than ancestors who fought in the Civil War—and no one ever calls her Poor Emily again.

Helen Mittermeyer begins her *Men of Ice* series
(continued)

with **QUICKSILVER,** LOVESWEPT #371. Helen is known for writing about strong, dangerous, enigmatic men, and hero Piers Larraby is all of those things. When gorgeous, silver-haired Damiene Belson appears from the darkness fleeing her pursuers, Piers is her sanctuary in the storm. But too many secrets threaten their unexpected love. You can count on Helen to deliver a dramatic story filled with romance.

Don't forget to start your holiday shopping early this year. Our LOVESWEPT Golden Classics featuring our Hometown Hunk winners are out in stores right now, and in the beginning of November you can pick up our lovely December LOVE-SWEPTs. They make great gifts. What could be more joyful than bringing a little romance into someone's life?

Best wishes,
Sincerely,

Carolyn Nichols

Carolyn Nichols
  Editor
LOVESWEPT
Bantam Books
666 Fifth Avenue
New York, NY 10103

FAN OF THE MONTH

Tricia Smith

I'm honored to have been chosen as a "fan of the month" for LOVESWEPT. A mother of two children with a house full of animals, I've been a romance reader for years. I was immediately captivated when I read the first LOVESWEPT book, **HEAVEN'S PRICE** by Sandra Brown. Ms. Brown is a very compelling author, along with so many of the authors LOVESWEPT has introduced into my life.

Each month I find myself looking forward to new adventures in reading with LOVESWEPT. The story lines are up-to-date, very well researched, and totally enthralling. With such fantastic authors as Iris Johansen, Kay Hooper, Fayrene Preston, Kathleen Creighton, Joan Elliott Pickart, and Deborah Smith, I'm always enchanted, from cover to cover, month after month.

I recently joined the Gold Coast Chapter of Romance Writers of America and have made wonderful friends who are all well-known authors as well as just great people. I hope to attend an RWA convention someday soon in order to meet the authors who've enriched my life in so many ways. Romance reading for me is not a pasttime but a passion.

THE DELANEY DYNASTY

Men and women whose loves an passions are so glorious it takes many great romance novels by three bestselling authors to tell their tempestuous stories.

THE SHAMROCK TRINITY

☐	21975	RAFE, THE MAVERICK *by Kay Hooper*	$2.95
☐	21976	YORK, THE RENEGADE *by Iris Johansen*	$2.95
☐	21977	BURKE, THE KINGPIN *by Fayrene Preston*	$2.95

THE DELANEYS OF KILLAROO

☐	21872	ADELAIDE, THE ENCHANTRESS *by Kay Hooper*	$2.75
☐	21873	MATILDA, THE ADVENTURESS *by Iris Johansen*	$2.75
☐	21874	SYDNEY, THE TEMPTRESS *by Fayrene Preston*	$2.75

THE DELANEYS: *The Untamed Years*

☐	21899	GOLDEN FLAMES *by Kay Hooper*	$3.50
☐	21898	WILD SILVER *by Iris Johansen*	$3.50
☐	21897	COPPER FIRE *by Fayrene Preston*	$3.50

Buy them at your local bookstore or use this page to order.

Bantam Books, Dept. SW7, 414 East Golf Road, Des Plaines, IL 60016

Please send me the items I have checked above. I am enclosing $_____
(please add $2.00 to cover postage and handling). Send check or money order, no cash or C.O.D.s please.

Mr/Ms _____

Address _____

City/State _____ Zip_____

Please allow four to six weeks for delivery.
Prices and availability subject to change without notice.

SW7–11/89

NEW!
Handsome Book Covers Specially Designed To Fit Loveswept Books

Our new French Calf Vinyl book covers come in a set of three great colors— royal blue, scarlet red and kachina green.

Each 7" × 9½" book cover has two deep vertical pockets, a handy sewn-in bookmark, and is soil and scratch resistant.

To order your set, use the form below.

Special Offer
Buy a Bantam Book
for only 50¢.

Now you can have Bantam's catalog filled with hundreds of titles plus take advantage of our unique and exciting bonus book offer. A special offer which gives you the opportunity to purchase a Bantam book for only 50¢. Here's how!

By ordering any five books at the regular price per order, you can also choose any other single book listed (up to a $5.95 value) for just 50¢. Some restrictions do apply, but for further details why not send for Bantam's catalog of titles today!

Just send us your name and address and we will send you a catalog!